From Amor to Zalm

Politics in British Columbia are unlike those in any other province. Everyone agrees on that. Not so well known, however, is the succession of distinctive — some would say eccentric — premiers who have guided the province since Confederation. *From Amor to Zalm* examines the careers of the most pivotal of these characters: Amor De Cosmos, who set the standard of eccentricity for those who followed him; Richard McBride, who sent B.C. lurching into the 20th century; W.A.C. Bennett, the man who set the course of B.C. politics for the past thirty-eight years. A fourth premier profiled in detail is little-known "Fighting Joe" Martin, who held office only briefly at the turn of the century. Martin did not have a profound effect on the history of the province, but was one of the most colourful men to hold the office anywhere in Canada. Other premiers dealt with in the book are J.F. McCreight, the first to hold the office, William Bowser, John Oliver, Duff Pattullo, Bill Bennett, Dave Barrett and Bill Vander Zalm.

From Amor to Zalm describes how these men reached the top and tries to explain why they behaved so strangely in office. It explores how the absence of a conventional party system and the image of British Columbia as the "last frontier" of Canada has affected its politics. The book points out that a materialism based on exploitation of the province's resources has until recently been uppermost in the minds of the voters and the politicians. Relations with Ottawa have always been dominated by demands for more federal funds despite B.C.'s abundant natural wealth.

This is a serious yet light-hearted look at a few of the eccentric characters who have been elected to the province's highest office.

After a thirty-year career as a newspaperman in Victoria, Peter Murray turned to the writing of regional history. His first book, *The Devil and Mr. Duncan,* was nominated for a B.C. Book Prize. *The Vagabond Fleet*, published in 1988, chronicles the controversy surrounding the North Pacific fur seal hunt based in Victoria. He also edited *Great Scott!*, a collection of newspaper columns by Jack Scott. All were published by Sono Nis Press of Victoria.

From Amor to Zalm

A Primer on B.C. Politics and its Wacky Premiers

Peter Murray

Orca Book Publishers

Canadian Cataloguing in Publication Data

Murray, Peter, 1928-
   From Amor to Zalm

   Includes bibliographical references.
   ISBN 0-9205-1-21-4 (bound). — ISBN 0-920501-26-5 (pbk.)

   1. Prime Ministers - British Columbia - Biography. 2. British
   Columbia - Politics and government.
I. Title.
FC3805.M87 1989   971.1'009'92   C86-091506-7   F1086.8.M87 1989

Orca Book Publishers
PO Box 5626, Stn. B
Victoria, B.C.
V8R 6S4
Canada

Publication assistance provided by the Canada Council.

Illustrations and cover design by Michael Wilkey.

Printed and bound in Canada by Hignell Printing Ltd.

To the memory of Torchy Anderson, a good friend and great newspaperman who had a knack for puncturing the stuffed shirts of politicians and others.

Contents

"I hate practically everything British Columbia stands for today — the shoddy, uncaring development of our natural resources, the Chamber of Commerce mentality which favors short-term material gain over all other considerations, the utter contempt for human values of every kind. I hate and despise the trivial provincial mentality that denies Canada's national heritage, which seeks petty advantage at cost to the common weal, which resists every vital Canadian concept and the whole range of modern knowledge and communication which can make the Canadian ideal a reality. I apologize to the rest of Canada for this narrow lack of faith and vision."

— Roderick Haig-Brown, June 21, 1965.

Chapter 1.

The Prodigal Province

Since British Columbia became a province in 1871, twenty-seven men have occupied the office of premier. Glancing down the list it is striking to see how many oddballs there have been among them. Even more remarkable is the fact that our most prominent and politically successful premiers have been, by Canadian provincial standards at least, among the most eccentric.

British Columbia has never been a province quite like the others. That it has never produced a national leader is not surprising. Try to imagine any of our leaders sitting at the federal cabinet table, let alone at its head. The image does not come readily to mind. Amor De Cosmos was a lonely backbencher in the House of Commons, which regarded him as a kind of exotic western bird. It is impossible to conceive of W. A. C. Bennett in Ottawa in any role. With his peculiar brand of populism that seems to flourish only in the hothouse of B.C. politics, he would never have been taken seriously in the larger arena.

Desmond Morton, a University of Toronto historian, questioned about Dave Barrett's chances in the 1989 national NDP leadership contest, pointed out that each region of Canada has a preferred style of premier. "Quebec likes *un chef*," Morton said, "someone who looks powerful and whacks people around; in Ontario it's somebody who is dull and responsible; in the Prairie west it's someone who is earnest; and in British Columbia it's somebody who's a little bit wingy."

I remember sitting in "Wacky" Bennett's office in the 1950s with a clutch of other newspapermen at one of the Premier's irregular press conferences. For Bennett it was a game. And a game for which he made the rules as he went along. For the rest of us it was a job. We were trying to extract information from a man forever beaming the self-satisfied grin of the Chesire Cat. He teased us with it like a grandfather doling out candies to the kids. We paid for every morsel that we got. In retrospect it seems a humiliating experience — including the long hours spent tossing pennies against the wall outside the cabinet room waiting for Bennett to emerge. When he did, we trotted after him down the stairs to his office door, desperately pleading for one of his goodies to convince the city editor we had been busy.

Bennett spoke to us only when there was political capital to be made. Providing the public with information about government was the last thing on his mind. At the time I was too young and inexperienced to question or criticize his obsessive secrecy. It was my first brush with politics and I assumed that was his prerogative as premier. There was no option but to play the game by his silly rules. It was years later, during research for this book in fact, before I became angry. As a newspaperman for the twenty years in which W.A.C. Bennett held office, I am ashamed of what he was allowed to do to the politics of the province.

I recall, too, the Legislative Press Gallery in the 1970s during the wild and woolly days when Dave Barrett, another grinning cherub like Bennett, was in office. The Opposition Leader then was Bill Bennett, a man forever struggling gamely to produce a smile for the cameras. It was painful to behold. The only time I ever saw him beam happily like his father was years later — the day he suddenly quit as premier in the middle of his third term. Then he looked like a man just let out of jail.

Barrett and the Bennetts made us an embarrassing national joke. Easterners think, not without cause, that the way British Columbians conduct their public business is zany. The latest and possibly the strangest in a long line of peculiar premiers, Bill Vander Zalm, has done nothing to alter that perception. And make no mistake — Vander Zalm is the natural progeny of the political forces set in motion by Amor de Cosmos and pushed along by Richard McBride, W.A.C. Bennett and others.

The blame for this state of affairs should not be laid on the premiers themselves. We, the voters, choose them after all. And in a few cases we re-elected them again and again, even after their failings had become painfully apparent. What is it about this province that pushes up such men and the voters who support them? A number of theories have been advanced which should be touched on lightly before examining the careers of some of British Columbia's more bizarre premiers.

● ● ●

Primary industries, particularly forestry, have long determined the economic climate of the province. Almost all of the premiers, and especially those profiled here, have acted out of a misguided vision of the province's future. They invariably saw its vast treasure house of natural resources as a vault to be looted. The environmental issues that in the 1980s began to concern the public as never before are the legacy of a long history of resource mismanagement.

The politics of economic expediency have resulted in a boom-and-bust economy in which the fortunes of communities have depended on world marketplaces. Bitter polarization between workers and bosses, free-enterprise politicians and their social democrat opponents has been the inevitable consequence. The province's riches have been the undoing of its leaders. The stability and political sanity of less-endowed provinces have eluded us.

When British Columbia decided, after a spirited debate, to join Confederation, it did so not in the spirit of completing the dream of a great nation spanning the continent. The Terms of Union were agreed to unsentimentally for the promise of economic gain. As Dr. J.S. Helmcken, a B.C. pioneer who opposed Confederation, put it: "No union between this colony (B.C.) and Canada can permanently exist unless it be to the material and pecuniary advantage of this colony to remain in the Union . . . the people of this colony have, generally speaking, no love for Canada . . . and care little or nothing about the distinctions between the form of Government of Canada and that of the United States . . . the only bond of union will be the material advantage of the country and pecuniary benefit of the inhabitants."

R.E. Gosnell, an editor, archivist, and historian who served as personal secretary to four premiers around the turn of the century, put it bluntly: "In the East the stimulus to Confederation was political and national, and was so in spite of local considerations (but) in British Columbia the conditions were entirely different . . . politically or socially, the influences of Eastern Canada did not extend to within a thousand miles of its extremest boundary eastward." In its physical contours and natural resources, the province "was in every sense foreign to Canada. Communication and trade were wholly with the Pacific Coast and Great Britain, and sympathies to a considerable extent followed in the line of trade and travel."

Small wonder then that, as a succession of its premiers held out their hands to Ottawa for more while boasting of the province's riches, British Columbia came to be regarded as the spoiled child of Confederation. Little has changed over the years. As historian Edwin R. Black has noted, "federal relations with the province have always been marked by disputes over money and economic control and little else."

Black notes "the notorious unpredictability" of B.C. premiers and the "tumultuousness of the partisan fray." There is "little sense of a common present, to say nothing of respect for a communal past." Traditional procedures act as restraints, and the action-oriented premiers and the majority of their constituents have had scant interest in anything that would impede the province's pell-mell rush for spoils.

This attitude has been a fact of life for the past century, ever since railway fever hit the province. Railroads were a symbol of progress everywhere, but British Columbia was the last area of the country to catch the disease. Millions of public dollars were squandered in land grants and subsidies in a desperate bid to "open up" the province. Scandal followed scandal as the land speculators had a field day. Voters eager for a piece of the action gave governments *carte blanche* to deal with the wheeler-dealers. The costly but blackly comic saga of the Pacific Great Eastern Railroad runs like a tangled thread through a succession of administrations.

British author J.B. Thornhill caught the essence of the place in his 1913 book, *British Columbia in the Making*: "The main idea . . . is to make money, and the only way to do this . . . is to exploit the resources of the country — to win the wealth that the soil, the sea, and the forest offer. Once the great financial centres of the world are satisfied that the dormant wealth is there, they are prepared to negotiate (and) make the best bargain they can."

Thornhill said there was easy money to be made selling real estate, which "offers splendid chances to swindlers." The voters of B.C. had totally different ideas to those of the older settled countries, and thought generally in terms of real estate, mines, forests and railways.

Things didn't change much over the years. Historian Margaret Ormsby wrote about the Vancouver of 1929: "The spirit of the city was still, as it had been at the beginning, predominantly materialistic. An eager, grasping, acquisitive community, it squandered all its own resources of natural beauty, all the time extending its economic power until it held most of the province in fee."

Twenty years later Attorney-General Gordon Wismer, praising his Coalition government for facilitating the giant Aluminum Company of Canada development at Kitimat, said: "The first thing a big company does is to look over resources. Second, and very near first, is the political climate." Corporations like Alcan have found that climate warm and accommodating.

Warnings that profligate use of the province's natural

resources could not continue forever have been consistently ignored. In 1939 the Rowell-Sirois Commission on Dominion-Provincial relations noted British Columbia's "highly concentrated corporate form of organization which has been adopted to exploit them." The report said "many of these resources are of a wasting character, and it has evidently been the Province's policy to secure a substantial share of the profits derived from their exploitation while it has the opportunity."

Maclean's magazine columnist Blair Fraser helped bring the Coalition government down in 1952 with his revelations of liquor licence corruption presided over by Wismer in Vancouver. He wrote that "some very odd things go on in B.C. politics, but they've been going on for years and nobody pays much attention." Fraser quoted an Ontario Tory: "Even in Quebec they wouldn't put up with the things that are tolerated in B.C."

• • •

On a trip to Ottawa in 1934 seeking more federal money, a familiar trek by British Columbia premiers, T. D. "Duff" Pattullo said the province "by reason of its diversity of interests, its salubrious climate and general attractiveness is the mecca of those who suffer from misfortunes, mischance or ill health." That has been a persistent theme in our history — B.C. as the last frontier, the final refuge for drifters from the rest of the country, a haven for ne'er-do-wells who gobble up our welfare budget.

A Chamber of Commerce view of the world has always reigned west of the Rockies, a land of Babbitts stuck in a time warp looking for the quick, easy buck. The Howe Street crapshoot with its flamboyant high-flyers who run the Vancouver Stock Exchange is an ideal symbol for the provincial economy.

Except for Dave Barrett, latter-day premiers of British Columbia have seldom read anything other than financial reports and political columns, although Vander Zalm does allow to perusing the odd gardening book. Pattullo once argued that Bruce Hutchison wrote better stuff than Shakespeare, adding, "or at least it's more interesting, and it's easier to read." Had they been more learned men, if only in the field of political history, they might have understood the values and traditions of the party system that keep democratic governments on a relatively even keel elsewhere. Political parties have rarely existed or functioned in a normal manner in British Columbia.

Richard McBride is generally credited with introducing party politics to the province at the turn of the century, but he was a Conservative in name only. Ever the opportunist, McBride simply responded to an electorate fed up with the shifting alliances and short-term expedience that marked the turbulent first thirty years of B.C. history. McBride was a pragmatist happy to oblige, but he did not have the least idea how to create and manage a party. He left his chief lieutenant, Attorney-General W.J. Bowser, to muddle through as best he could.

A party system of sorts existed for the next thirty years, although the Liberals and Tories had exactly the same policies in terms of their views on the major issues of the day: economic expansion, railway building, and Oriental immigration. The two parties simply took turns switching places from the government to the opposition side of the legislature until the emergence during the Depression of the Co-operative Commonwealth Federation (CCF). This new party of the left was accepted in federal politics and in a number of provinces, but in B.C. it was regarded with fear and loathing by business leaders and the political establishment from the very beginning.

At about the same time the CCF was born, a group of Vancouver businessmen headed by timber tycoon H.R. MacMillan urged the Conservative government of the day to launch a study of government finances and recommend possible changes. Premier Simon Fraser Tolmie duly complied, appointing, not surprisingly, five businessmen to carry out the task. Their report condemned the party system outright, blaming it for budget deficits brought about by the extravagance of patronage and welfare. ''An efficient and unhampered administrative machine'' was required to replace outmoded legislative government, it said.

To his credit, Tolmie, an otherwise weak premier, blanched at the idea of Mussolini-style government in B.C. and rejected the report. He did, however, issue a call for a "Union Government" of all parties during the period of economic crisis. This first attempt at a coalition failed when it was rejected by both the CCF and Liberals. Less than ten years later, however, Tolmie's Liberal successor, Duff Pattullo, was forced out of office by the same business interests and replaced by a coalition of Grits and Tories whose object was simply to keep the CCF out. Normal party politics were finished in the province after a relatively brief fling, and have never returned.

After a decade of uneasy alliance, the Coalition was given the *coup de grace* by one of its own disgruntled members, W.A.C. Bennett. Although the Kelowna hardware merchant had been an enthusiastic supporter of the idea in the beginning, he eventually found his personal ambitions for leadership frustrated. Coalition governments, by their very nature, have a way of doing that.

Bennett solved his problem by hijacking the Social Credit League of British Columbia, a motley collection of monetary crackpots and idealists, and turning it into his personal political vehicle. (Major C.H. Douglas, the British engineer who devised the theory of Social Credit, died in 1952 just as Bennett was wheeling into power.) The claim that Bennett created a new political party does not bear scrutiny. Social Credit is simply the old Coalition in new clothes. The business community which had created the original Coalition to keep the CCF/NDP from power turned to the Socreds for the same purpose.

Jack Clarke, a columnist for the Vancouver *Province*, a newspaper which staunchly supported Social Credit at election time for thirty-five years, described the new grouping as a collection of "malcontents, castoffs from other parties and ambitious careerists united by a single bond — their fear of socialism." For the average voter, Clarke said, it was easier to fear socialism than Social Credit, despite the anti-Semite ghosts and other claptrap in the Socred closet.

Asked to define his version of Social Credit, Bennett replied simply that it was "the opposite of socialism." So much for the claim that it is a political party. The reality was underscored by such Social Credit election slogans as, "Progress, not Politics" and Bennett's insistence that it was a "movement," not a party. If there were any lingering doubts on that score Bennett wiped them aside when he declared that "in this province we are not divided into parties . . . we are simply divided into two clear groups: those who believe in British Columbia and those who don't."

The Bennett version of Social Credit was less idealistic than its earlier counterpart in Alberta, where it was born of Depression rather than prosperity. Historian Martin Robin has written that "the genius of B.C. Social Credit lies in its ability to manipulate, rather than eliminate, group conflict and resentment." Such are the politics of confrontation that have gripped the province for lo these many years.

Liberal Pat McGeer, later a convert to Social Credit when he found no other outlet for his ambition, summed it up best: "The political equation in British Columbia is basic — and crude. The economy is resource oriented, dependent on a free flow of foreign capital into the province. Expressed in political terms, that means a free-enterprise government. The spectre at the feast is socialism." McGeer wrote in 1972: "In election after election since 1952, this formula has been parlayed into a continuing Social Credit majority. It has happened in the face of events that would certainly have toppled governments elsewhere in the country." Three years later McGeer surrendered to the inevitable and joined the winners. His abrupt apostasy symbolized the cynicism that has corrupted B.C. politics over the years.

Amor De Cosmos

Chapter 2.

The Cosmic Man

Asked who was the first Premier of British Columbia, the name John Foster McCreight does not come tripping to the tongue. Like a number of premiers who succeeded him over the next century, McCreight rests in deserved obscurity.

When he took office on November 13, 1871, the citizenry wondered what McCreight had done to deserve such an honour. He was chosen not by the voters, or even members of the Legislative Assembly, but by the autocratic new Lieutenant-Governor, Joseph Trutch.

As Commissioner of Lands, Trutch had been a strong figure in the colonial administration. He had been rewarded with the first lieutenant-governorship by a federal cabinet grateful for his concessions allowing it to renege on some rash railway promises to the budding province. Once in the driver's seat, Trutch intended to keep the same tight control over the new province as James Douglas had earlier for the Hudson's Bay Company.

McCreight, 44, a lawyer who had shown little interest in political affairs, was the kind of man Trutch was looking for. He was not likely to make trouble like those rabble-rousers in the Assembly such as newspaper editor Amor De Cosmos. McCreight wasn't keen on responsible government and had not been a supporter of Confederation.

It was not that McCreight was a milquetoast. A steely-eyed, humourless Irishman with a biting tongue and hot temper, he was considered to be a moody, aloof snob, a hard but unconvivial drinker. It was said that his closest friend was his horse "Tally," on whom he lavished great care each day. With his odd mix of courtliness and blunt candour, J. F. McCreight was the first in a long line of eccentric premiers.

McCreight had a reputation as a bit of a brawler. In 1861, two years after arriving in the city, he tangled with Dr. William Rumsey. De Cosmos' *British Colonist* reported gleefully that the two men had met outside the Brown Jug Saloon, the hub of Victoria at Fort and Government Streets. Angry words were exchanged. A crowd gathered and watched as Rumsey was felled with a well-aimed blow to the head. When a friend of the doctor intervened, he met the same fate. According to the *Colonist*, McCreight lashed out at a few others before retiring from the field. The next day McCreight appeared in police court charged with assault, pleaded guilty and was fined $25. (In later years De Cosmos himself would appear from time to time on the police blotter for similar offences.)

The cause of the altercation was never determined. McCreight had recently appeared for Rumsey, however, at an inquest which cleared him in the death of a town drunk said to have died from an overdose of laudanum administered by the doctor.

McCreight was regarded as a purist about the law in a province where legal niceties were often winked at. So it is not surprising that he clashed with Chief Justice Matthew Baillie Begbie, an enforcer of his own unique version of frontier justice.

In a community that took great delight in gossip, McCreight's private life was a subject of intense speculation. He was secretive about his young wife, Elizabeth Ann, who seldom appeared in Victoria society and is said to have ended her days in a San Francisco asylum.

It was a cause for celebration when McCreight gave up as premier after only thirteen months in office, letting it be known he was fed up with the machinations expected of a politician. He was appointed to the bench, where he later became the target rather than the perpetrator of an assault. A peppery young lawyer, recently arrived from the East, became frustrated by McCreight's crankiness during a Chambers hearing and hurled a heavy glass ink pot in the judge's direction.

Only in his oddities did McCreight resemble the twenty-six premiers who have followed him. He made little impact and left no mark on the province, an easily forgettable figure.

● ● ●

Not so his successor, who set a high standard for eccentricity by which the others can be measured.

He was born William Alexander Smith on August 25, 1825, one of ten children of Jesse and Charlotte Smith, in Windsor, N.S. When the family moved to Halifax in 1840 in search of a better life, young Willie took a clerical job with a wholesale grocery firm. He stuck with it for the next ten years.

Like many other aspects of Smith's life, little is known of this period. Although he later became a prolific newspaper writer, Smith apparently kept no diary or journal and wrote few if any letters. It is known that he was interested in politics in Halifax, becoming an ardent admirer of Joseph Howe, a newspaperman who led the fight in the Maritimes for responsible government. Howe was a noted orator and the young clerk was inspired by his platform style. Smith became involved in the Dalhousie College Debating Club and attended night classes at a grammar school conducted by John Thompson, whose son later became Prime Minister. Smith also took an interest in the new science of photography.

At age twenty-six, Smith suddenly pulled up stakes to set out for the California gold-fields and new opportunities. Unlike the majority of Easterners who went West at this time, he set out by land. Most young men, including his older brother Charles two years later, travelled by boat to Central America, crossed overland to the Pacific and caught another ship for San Francisco.

The wagon route chosen by William Smith was fraught with danger, from both the elements and hostile Indians. After reaching Salt Lake City safely, he decided to spend some time in the Mormon community recently established by Brigham Young. Smith was impressed by the achievements of these industrious people and apparently used his business experience to become involved in some trading ventures. He earned enough money to buy his first camera.

It is not known to what extent Smith became involved with the Mormon Church. Later, in Victoria, he was sometimes jeered at as "Mormon Bill," but there is no evidence that he ever was a member of the sect. Smith did become active in the Masonic Order in California, however, and later in Victoria for a time. He always had an interest in current theological issues and disputes. Opposed to the established churches, he was a freethinker who questioned dogma and fought the established "church monopoly" in Victoria and the province. He vigorously objected to the ban on Sunday trade.

After his year at Salt Lake, Smith set off again with a wagon train bound for Sacramento. Impatient with the slow pace of the caravan, he struck out on his own by horseback through the rough terrain of the Sierra Nevadas.

In California, after his camera arrived with the caravan, Smith settled in the little mining camp settlement of Mud Springs (later to become the more glamorous El Dorado, "City of Gold") where he established a business taking photographs of mining claims which could be used as evidence in disputes over claim-jumping. As he travelled around the state, Smith also dabbled in land speculation.

Then, just as Mud Springs attempted to improve its image by a change of name, Smith decided to do the same. His choice of Amor De Cosmos, with the three components taken respectively from Latin, French and Greek, was a curious one. He said at the time there were too many Bill Smiths around the mining camps and since there were no streets or numbers, his mail was constantly being misdirected. Others have suggested that Smith was attempting to make a new beginning in his life, a change of identity symbolized by a bizarre new name.

Whatever the real reason, Smith's petition for a legal change of name was the cause of merriment when it reached the floor of the California legislature. It passed through the state senate with relative ease after being brought forward by Sen. Gavin D. Hall, who Smith had retained as his lawyer. But in the House a number of Assemblymen could not resist making fun of this strange request. One amendment would have rechristened Smith "Amor Muggins Cosmos," another "Amor De Cosmos Caesar." One member objected to the "De" as being too aristocratic for frontier California. Another suggested that Smith merely hoped to impress the ladies with a more romantic name. (In view of his life-long bachelorhood and apparent disinterest in the opposite sex, this charge was obviously unfounded).

In the face of such ridicule, Smith wrote an Assemblyman: "I desire not to adopt the name of Amor De Cosmos because it smacks of a foreign title, but because it is an unusual name and its meaning tells what I love most, viz: Love of order, beauty, the world, the universe."

After more frivolous debate, a vote was taken and the petition approved 41 to 20. On February, 17, 1854, William Alexander Smith became, at the age of twenty-eight, forevermore, Amor De Cosmos. Until that decisive day in an ordinary life, the man behind the name Smith had failed to make any mark on the world. Soon, whether by coincidence or not, he would become a force to be reckoned with in the affairs of British Columbia and Canada. (In this regard he more or less defied the maxim of the British writer M.F. Tupper that "few men have grown unto greatness whose names are allied to ridicule." De Cosmos did however have to endure being referred to mockingly as "cupid" and "love of order Smith.")

De Cosmos made his first trip to Victoria on the steamer *Brother Jonathan* in May of 1858, liked what he saw, and returned to California to wind up his affairs. He was back on Vancouver Island before the end of June.

As both Smith and De Cosmos he had spent seven years in the United States but never took any steps toward gaining American citizenship. (It was later rumoured that he had declared his intention to do so in order to facilitate his change of name). Nor, despite the interest he had shown in Halifax, did he take an active role in California politics. The entire episode, like many others in his life, is shrouded in mystery on which he never attempted to shed any light.

• • •

After settling in British Columbia De Cosmos wasted little time before becoming involved in business and social affairs. It was an exciting, expansive time in the history of the colony and he was quick to see the opportunities. He was joined in some of these endeavours by his brother Charles, with whom he had teamed up in California in 1854 before both men moved north back to their native country at about the same time.

De Cosmos did not restrict his early activities to British Columbia. Less than a month after his arrival he boarded the steamer *Leviathan* for Semiahmoo in Washington Territory, between the modern border towns of Blaine and Bellingham. He told the only other passenger, Victoria newspaperman and entrepreneur David Higgins, that he intended to check out the area's commercial possibilities as a rival of Victoria. There was a certain amount of speculation at the time in coal deposits in the area. There is no evidence, however, that De Cosmos made any investments there. More important was the contact with Higgins, who found the newcomer an agreeable companion. De Cosmos invited him to join his venture of establishing the first newspaper in Victoria later in the year. De Cosmos had chosen his future career.

Meanwhile, De Cosmos purchased a number of lots in Victoria, Esquimalt and at Fort Langley in the lower Fraser Valley on the basis of Governor Douglas' decision to make it the capital of the new mainland colony. When Col. R. C. Moody later persuaded Douglas that a site on the Fraser River at New Westminster was more suitable, De Cosmos and other speculators were allowed to return their lots to the government in exchange for others at the new townsite.

Having become a Freemason in California, De Cosmos wasted no time establishing the order in Victoria. On July 12 at a meeting in Southgate's Store he and a number of leading businessmen founded the first lodge in Victoria. De Cosmos adroitly used the contacts made through Masonry in his early newspapering and political career, until he decided he needed it no longer and left in 1865.

The *British Colonist* made its debut on December 11, 1858, with De Cosmos ensconced in the editor's chair. The fact that he had arrived in the colony just six months before, and had no previous newspaper experience, did not daunt him. De Cosmos came out swinging in the first edition against Governor James Douglas' patriarchal administration.

It was hardly surprising that the Nova Scotia democrat would clash with the autocratic H.B.C. officer. When Douglas had been ordered by London in 1856 to set up a Legislative Assembly in the colony, he decreed that its members must own $1,500 of free-hold property and voters must have twenty acres. The Governor declared himself "utterly averse to a universal franchise."

De Cosmos roasted Douglas in his second edition for presiding over an administration marked by "toadyism, consanguinity, and incompetency, compounded with white-washed Englishmen and renegade Yankees." De Cosmos never minced words, either as editor or legislator, and his enemies became legion.

Douglas retorted that De Cosmos was a white-washed American who must have been a United States citizen in order to get his name changed. The editor dismissed that sally as a "malignant, envious, black-hearted lie." Douglas had not experienced such insolence from his subjects before, and responded rashly. He demanded that the *Colonist* post a $3,000 "good behaviour" bond or shut down its presses, an old but by then discredited way of dealing with the upstart press in England. De Cosmos could not have asked for more. He revelled in the role of martyr and closed the newspaper's doors on April 2, 1859. Many of the town's businessmen and new arrivals, already chafing under Douglas' autocratic ways, were outraged. A public meeting was called and the bond money was enthusiastically subscribed. The *Colonist* was back on the street within a week of suspending publication.

When the newspaper began, it was a four-page weekly selling for twelve and a half cents (a "bit") or $5 a year, with a circulation of only two hundred. After the initial row with Douglas, the paper went to three editions a week. The following year De Cosmos was called before the bar of the Legislative Assembly accused of libelling the Speaker, Dr. J.S. Helmcken. He gave the demanded apology and promptly made the *Colonist* a daily. Within a year he was printing four thousand copies. The paper's heady mix of pungent editorial comment and salty gossip contributed to its success.

But De Cosmos was not content with sniping from the sidelines of political battle. He longed to get into the fray. In 1860 he was one of three candidates in the two-seat Victoria riding. He placed third following an extraordinary decision by Attorney-General George Hunter Cary, another of the candidates, to extend the franchise to black immigrants from the U.S. Cary decreed they were eligible to vote despite the fact they had been in Victoria less than two years and were not yet citizens. The Attorney-General shrewdly surmised that these refugees from discrimination would regard De Cosmos as a transplanted American and would tip the scales by voting against him, which they apparently did.

It was a boisterous campaign. Victorians regarded politics as entertainment, and Cary and De Cosmos delivered a first-class show in a campaign meeting at a city theatre. The audience cheered, hissed and shouted as the two men slashed verbally at each other. Cary was wildly excitable by nature, while De Cosmos enhanced his performance with liquor. He struck a number of dramatic poses, including a boast that he had travelled throughout California with a revolver in each boot.

When De Cosmos tried again later that year in an Esquimalt by- election, Cary, a solid Establishment man, found another way to thwart the editor's ambitions. This time he insisted that De Cosmos' name appear on the ballot as "Smith, commonly known as De Cosmos," a ploy that succeeded when the potential tying vote was cast erroneously for simply "De Cosmos." Finally, in his third try, De Cosmos was elected in Victoria in a general election July 20, 1863.

Two months later Douglas announced that he was retiring from public life. Within two weeks, De Cosmos let it be known he was selling the *Colonist* to the staff in order to devote full time to politics. Election to the Assembly and the loss of his old foe as a target left little reason for hanging on to the newspaper. His goals had been met: elective office for himself and the start of responsible government for the colony. Now he would become the stormy petrel of the province's early politics, leading the opposition against the lingering remnants of the old ways. A rabble-rousing speaker, he kept the public opinion pot boiling. De Cosmos set British Columbia on a free-wheeling, populist course that it has followed more or less to the present day.

● ● ●

De Cosmos had three main interests at this time: union of the mainland and Vancouver colonies, confederation with the rest of Canada, and finally, responsible government. Union was achieved within three years, involving the temporary selection of New Westminster as the capital, but the Confederation debate was long and bitter and responsible government slow in coming.

A natural haughtiness was brought to bear by De Cosmos on his colleagues in the Assembly. He once referred to the Legislative Chamber as the "Provincial Menagerie" in which "debates partook more of the character of a lot of Bavarians after they had swallowed the sixtieth glass of lager." The members' lack of knowledge or appreciation of parliamentary principles was an object of De Cosmos' scorn. With his Nova Scotia background and wide reading, he considered himself superior to all. He had an ally for a time in fellow newspaperman John Robson, but they soon came to a parting of the ways. Most of De Cosmos' alliances eventually unravelled. He was a loner, politically and socially.

The Colonial Secretary in Victoria, Philip Hankin,

summed up the official view of De Cosmos in a despatch to his superiors in London: "He is a thorough democratic ruffian . . . a great nuisance in the House, and abuses the officials and the government generally."

One of the officials ruffled by De Cosmos was Joseph Despard Pemberton, the crusty colonial surveyor-general. Both ended up in police court in June of 1859 on a charge of breaching the peace after trading blows on a downtown street. The two men were freed on condition they avoid each other's company for the next twelve months.

From the outset of his legislative career De Cosmos battled with Speaker Helmcken, son-in-law of James Douglas and a leader of the Old Guard. Helmcken did his best to stifle De Cosmos' caustic tongue and forced him to apologize to the Chair on more than one occasion for his heated outbursts.

De Cosmos found ways to fight with even his few allies. One was Dr. John Ash, a reform advocate who often sided with De Cosmos in Assembly debates. On a spring day in 1866 the two men met outside after differing over a legislative issue. They argued and De Cosmos lashed out at Ash with a walking stick he often carried, breaking the doctor's glasses and drawing blood. Ash was stronger than his tall but slender assailant and began pummelling him. Ash appeared about to heave De Cosmos over the James Bay bridge into the harbour when passersby, including Helmcken, separated the combatants. The *Daily Chronicle*, edited by D.W. Higgins, by now a harsh critic of De Cosmos, lamented smugly the following day that "We have here another instance of this miserable man's unfitness to represent respectable people."

By 1868, when another general election was called, the respectable people of Victoria did indeed decide they had had enough of De Cosmos and his erratic ways. And once again he was the victim of electoral chicanery. In this instance Governor Frederick Seymour, urged on, it was said, by Helmcken, allowed all residents other than Indians or Chinese to vote. Dropping the previous requirements of British citizenship and property ownership allowed the numerous Americans in the colony to alter the voting balance. Not only were the majority of the Americans fervently opposed to confederation, but actually favoured annexation of the colony to the United States.

The annexation movement flourished for a time, but within a year the confederation forces had regrouped and sympathy swung back to union with Canada. De Cosmos himself won by a large majority in a byelection in December of 1869. When it was decided to send a delegation to Ottawa to negotiate terms, however, De Cosmos was left at home. The two leading figures of the team were Helmcken and Joseph Trutch. Helmcken, who had mellowed somewhat toward De Cosmos but was still lukewarm about confederation, proposed that either De Cosmos or Robson go in his place, but Trutch rejected both.

In frustration at being left out of the vital negotiations with the federal government, De Cosmos started another newspaper to provide an additional forum for his views. The *Daily Standard*, which he dubbed "The People's Paper," made its first appearance June 20, 1870. While the delegation was in Ottawa, the *Standard* pressed hard for favourable terms for the province's admission to union, including responsible government. De Cosmos was furious when it was learned that the delegation had accepted a temporary Legislative Council made up of nine elected members and six to be appointed by the Lieutenant-Governor. He noted that the previous Assembly was a fully elected body, even though its powers were limited.

On July 20, 1871, the fateful day arrived: British Columbia became a province of Canada. Although he lost out to Trutch for the coveted post of first Lieutenant-Governor, De Cosmos rejoiced in the successful outcome of his long campaign and delivered the most stirring speech at a gala public picnic celebrating the event.

A grateful citizenry elected him at the head of the poll in October to the new twenty-five-member elected Legislative Assembly. In the following month De Cosmos was also elected one of the two Victoria members in the Dominion Parliament. He saw no conflict in holding the two elective offices at the same time. Meanwhile, he used the columns of the *Standard* to flay Premier McCreight and his weak-kneed cabinet for knuckling under to Trutch.

But rather than stay to fight in the Assembly, De Cosmos left in February of 1872 to take his seat in the House of Commons. His brother Charles took control of the *Standard*.

When the McCreight administration finally collapsed in December, Trutch, embarrassed by the failure of his hand-picked man, suffered further distress when he found himself with no other practical choice than De Cosmos to take his place.

• • •

Although this should have been the crowning achievement of De Cosmos' career, he took no apparent satisfaction in the post of premier. He was the leader of an undistinguished administration which lasted only fourteen months. In the mold of John Diefenbaker and many another quarrelsome politician, the combative De Cosmos was happiest and most effective in opposition. These men function best as critics, not leaders. De Cosmos seemed unable to work congenially with others and so accomplished little.

He hung on to his seat in Ottawa and often showed more interest in federal affairs, leaving most of the work at home to Attorney-General George Anthony Walkem, who had held the same position under McCreight and later became premier himself. It is worth noting that De Cosmos' former sparring partner, Dr. Ash, was offered and accepted a cabinet post. De Cosmos may have been irascible and wrathful, but he did not hold grudges.

His first move as premier was to humble Trutch. The Lieutenant-Governor had been in the habit of sitting in on McCreight's cabinet meetings, but the new premier let Trutch know from the start that he was no longer welcome at such sessions.

De Cosmos took office at a time when the province, particularly Victoria, was going through a period of tough financial times following the collapse of the Cariboo gold mines. The failure of the federal government to meet its deadlines on construction of a railroad to the coast, thereby holding up economic opportunities, added to the frustrations of the populace.

The Premier became the target of this discontent at a public meeting in Victoria February 7, 1873, attended by eight hundred people, including many of his old Establishment foes. The tone of the meeting turned ugly when a rumour reached the hall that at that very moment the Assembly was considering changes in the terms of union. It was immediately decided to adjourn and march across the bridge to the "Birdcage" buildings which housed the legislators. Singing "We'll hang old De Cosmos on a sour apple tree" to the tune of the "Battle Hymn of the Republic" as they walked, the mob soon swelled to an estimated two thousand people.

Arriving at the Bar of the House they presented a threatening sight. The Speaker, Dr. James Trimble, fled the chamber to the safety of his office, followed closely behind by the cowering De Cosmos. The mob shouted "tyrant" and "traitor" at the Premier as they milled about.

To answer his critics, De Cosmos a year later called another public meeting, which turned out to be equally disastrous. The mood was rowdy as more than a thousand people crowded into Philarmonic Hall. They greeted De Cosmos with hisses and jeers. Because of the commotion, the Premier could not speak for several minutes. When he succeeded in making himself heard briefly, he defended his record and declared that his administration was the most honest in the province's history — which wasn't saying much since it was only the second. Hecklers taunted him as a "traitor" who had "sold us out." They called him "Mormon Bill," and he in turn labelled his tormentors hoodlums, scum and skunks. De Cosmos began to bellow at the crowd that they were the "vilest scum of the earth."

Despite his rude reception, ten days later, on January 22, 1874, De Cosmos was re-elected to the Commons. On February 4 he abruptly resigned as premier and gave up his seat in the Assembly, a step now required by law if he wanted to remain a member of Parliament. That was still De Cosmos' first choice, especially after the humiliation suffered at the hands of the mob.

British Columbians had not taken to the party system and politics were volatile and unpredictable. Although party government did take hold for a time in the province at the turn of the century, politics here have seldom conformed to the practices of the other provinces.

●　●　●

In Ottawa, De Cosmos spoke rarely and made no impact on national issues. He continued to work on behalf of his province, but had little success in these endeavours either. He complained that ten years after B.C. had joined Confederation, "not a pick has been struck in the ground in the way of construction, not a shovel full of earth has been lifted, not a cartful of earth or stone has been carried, not a culvert has been built, not a bridge erected, not a tie laid, not a rail stretched — nothing has been done whatever."

It was a cry against against Ottawa's cold-heartedness toward the West that has echoed for more than a century since. At one point, De Cosmos went so far as to introduce a half-hearted resolution in the Commons calling for separation of the province from Canada.

Such gestures ensured his continuing popularity at home and he was reelected easily in the general election of 1878. His career as a political maverick in Ottawa would continue for a few more years. There is little doubt he wanted to represent B.C. in the federal cabinet, but neither John A. Macdonald nor Alexander Mackenzie would take a chance on a radical unwilling to abide by the conventional political rules of compromise and patience.

Racial bigotry was commonplace at the time, but its vigorous expression by a man whose name proclaimed him to be a lover of the universe was a dismaying example of the sham involved in his pose. De Cosmos had no sympathy for the Indians whose way of life had been uprooted by the whites and who clustered in camps around Victoria in the summer months. He regarded them as a "moral pest" and "social ulcer" responsible for rampant prostitution and violence along the road to Esquimalt. They should be kept forcibly in their villages, he declared.

Chinese and blacks also felt the sting of De Cosmos' pen and tongue. He tolerated the Chinese as long as they were required for cheap menial labour, but believed they should be shipped back to China when their usefulness was ended. He objected to the amounts of money sent by the men back home to their families, while at the same time he opposed their being allowed to buy land here. His political foes at home noted, however, that De Cosmos derived some of his income from owning rented shanties in Victoria's Chinatown.

In his last years in the House of Commons, De Cosmos became almost obsessional on the subject. By this time he did not want the Chinese to work even on the transcontinental railway, and urged the government to undertake the project itself rather than have private contractors who relied on their indentured labour. A motion he submitted to block the Chinese from landing in Canada was ruled out of order because of treaty commitments with China. The ingenious De Cosmos then supported a move to ban men with hair longer than eight inches working on railroad construction. (All Chinese men wore queues at that time and could not return to China without them.) He got nowhere with these measures, however. Sir John A. Macdonald said it was "simply a question of Chinese labour or no railway."

De Cosmos' hostility to blacks may have had its origins in his years in the United States, but reached the depths of bigotry after his electoral defeat at their hands in Victoria. In an editorial following the vote he referred to them as "a lowborn, secretly banded, prejudiced race of aliens." It was wrong, he wrote, that "Englishmen should be slaves to escaped slaves." The fraudulent election had been "committed by a degraded race, who are banded together — who can never amalgamate with us — ignorant of self-government, of British institutions." De Cosmos was heard to say soon after that he would "drive the damned niggers from the colony."

De Cosmos eventually lost the support of the Victoria voters, especially after declaring in the Commons that Canada should break away from Britain and become an independent nation. That was further than even his most ardent supporters were prepared to go, and they tossed him out of office in the election of July 1882. And so his public life ended at the age of fifty-seven.

Normally after such a prominent career a politician could expect to be rewarded with some sinecure such as appointment to the Senate or Lieutenant-Governor, but the man known as Amor de Cosmos was not so honoured. He had played by his own rules, had no cronies in high places, nor left any political debts to be paid. And so he drifted into obscurity, embittered by his rejection and neglect. But De Cosmos did not go gently into his dark night.

At first he turned his attention to his widespread financial interests. The *Colonist* reported as early as 1873 that his "favorite exclamation" was "to ---- with the people! I've worked long enough for them — I'm now going to work for me."

In 1883 De Cosmos launched a lawsuit to recover the cost of trips made on behalf of the province to Ottawa and London in 1881. A judge ruled that he had a right to some compensation but no legal right to the large amount he claimed. *The Colonist* said he had visited Rome, Paris, Pompeii and the Holy Land, and had put in for everything, including tips.

De Cosmos was as secretive about his business dealings as he was about all other aspects of his private life, but it is known that he was president of a railway company in the late 1880's which proposed to operate between Victoria and Sidney and then by ferry across the Gulf of Georgia to New Westminster. As late as 1890 he was also involved in large real estate deals. His commercial holdings in Victoria, including a number of valuable building lots on Yates Street, made him financially independent. His major investments were in mineral prospects, timber, fishing and real estate.

It was his interest in mining that landed De Cosmos in the most embarrassing scandal of his career — the Texada Island affair. Not surprisingly, it began with an article by his arch-foe David Higgins early in 1874 soon after his resignation as premier. Higgins said he had learned that De Cosmos and a number of other prominent men had made a secret trip to the south end of Texada Island in the Gulf of Georgia the previous year to check out an iron ore deposit which they planned to sell to British investors. At the urging of John Robson, a Royal Commission headed by Chief Justice Begbie was set up to investigate. De

Cosmos later expressed his fury at Robson by telling the Commission that while he was "never angry and seldom agitated . . . if it had not been for that damned scoundrel I should not have been put to the expense of coming here." He waved his cane threateningly at Robson as he spoke.

The evidence was conflicting but De Cosmos admitted he hoped to make a small commission as an agent in the sale of the property. He said his main interest was in securing the first iron mine in the province. Begbie concluded in his report that while there were "circumstances apparently suspicious," the allegations of corruption had not been proved. He criticized De Cosmos, however, for failing to discriminate between his duties as premier and his rights as a private citizen. Although he had been cleared, suspicions about De Cosmos' role in the Texada affair lingered on.

As the years slipped by, De Cosmos began the pathetic descent from eccentricity into madness. Increasingly reclusive, he became morose and liable to lose control when he had been drinking. Encountering Robert Dunsmuir and Roderick Finlayson in front of the Bank of British Columbia in 1885, he made an insulting remark to Dunsmuir. Mayor R.P. Rithet was similarly treated when he approached. De Cosmos hit Dunsmuir on the side of the head with his fist and Dunsmuir retaliated by swinging his furled umbrella. Some who looked on said later that De Cosmos appeared to have been drunk.

A gaunt, haggard figure, he walked the streets in his frock coat, silk hat and walking stick. With his pale countenance and slender, delicate hands he had the look of an aesthete rather than a brawler. De Cosmos never rode the new street-cars because of an obsessive fear of electricity, refusing even to have it in his home. His beard was said to be kept black with shoe polish. He had the odd habit of staring intently at passersby, but not speaking. Adults were made uncomfortable and children frightened. Some compared him to the evil Svengali in the then current novel *Trilby*.

In 1890 De Cosmos erected a barbed wire fence across Pandora Street, claiming part of it as his private property. Mayor Grant complained bitterly that "it would be better for the community were Mr. De Cosmos outside it. Mr De Cosmos is a peculiarly objectionable man and ought to be ostracized.''

Three years later De Cosmos was at war with the city again, attempting to prevent the telephone company from erecting poles in front of one of his properties, appealing his tax assessment, and inserting a notice in the *Colonist* informing the public that he would barricade Camosun, Johnson and Pandora Streets for six hours in order to establish his claims to ownership of part of them.

In 1895, after making a feeble effort to return to politics, De Cosmos was reported to be subject to ''violent hallucinations.'' After an official examination he was declared to be of unsound mind. His brother took over his affairs. Two years later, on July 4, 1897, De Cosmos died. His estate included $117,000 in real estate, of which $87,000 was mortgaged.

Only a handful of people were present for his funeral service and burial in Ross Bay Cemetery. His old antagonist J.S. Helmcken in a letter to the *Colonist* lamented the fact that De Cosmos' former friends and allies did not attend the funeral. Beaumont Boggs, a friend of De Cosmos and a reporter on the *Standard* regretted that ''he lived too long.''

● ● ●

While De Cosmos' public career is open to scrutiny, any attempt to capsulize the private man, to hunt for the well-springs of his motivations and actions, proves more difficult. His soaring ambition and drive for power came from hidden sources. Two biographers, working with the most limited of materials, have failed to bring him to life, to explain his often erratic course. Unless more information is uncovered, which seems unlikely now, the task is probably impossible. Amor De Cosmos, in keeping with his strange choice of a new name, will remain an enigma.

It is possible, however, by examining the descriptions and reactions of some his more observant contemporaries to reach some conclusions about the man and fix his place as the forerunner of the other offbeat characters who have held the office of premier in this offbeat province.

An emotional man, De Cosmos often let tears flow in public. At least two other premiers who followed him, John Oliver and W.A.C. Bennett, shared this trait.

One man who knew De Cosmos well over a long period of time and recognized both his strong and weak points, was Gilbert M. Sproat, pioneer lumberman and Indian Agent. Sproat considered De Cosmos to be a master of details, an omnivorous reader always pursuing knowledge. Informed and clever, he had no controlling wisdom. De Cosmos was clear and forceful as a speaker but lacked the eloquence and the warmth or wit to inspire an audience. His speeches were often over-loaded with detail, while his writing was forceful but not graceful. De Cosmos harboured great ambitions but was too impulsive to achieve his goals in a thorough, orderly way.

David Higgins concluded that De Cosmos would have achieved greater success "had he been less emotional and more conciliatory." Higgins displayed his own vitriolic manner in labelling De Cosmos as a reformer with a "restless disposition ever in search of some new thing. In politics he is the revolutionary, the leveller, the wild experimenter . . . in religion he is a scoffer, a sceptic, a socialist — possibly a Mormon!"

After being described by the *Standard* as "an outcast from the scum of the lowest dens of New York," Higgins retorted with equal venom that De Cosmos, "either ashamed of his parentage or his crimes at Salt Lake, dropped his patronymic and assumed the name of Amor De Cosmos, the more effectually perhaps, to preserve himself from punishment." It was the kind of mud-slinging that makes today's newspapers seem namby-pamby. Nobody worried about libel suits in those rollicking times.

A century later the editor of the left-wing *Pacific Tribune* tried to claim De Cosmos as one of them, "a sort of socialist," as Helmcken also once described him. But De Cosmos was too much the land speculator and financial opportunist ever to fit that label.

He was a kind of Don Quixote always in need of some windmill to tilt. That explains why his greatest success was as a newspaperman rather than a politician. His most lasting contribution was to open up the colony to the expression of free opinion.

The difficulty in pinning De Cosmos down is emphasized by the rich variety and range of adjectives used by writers down the years to describe him: Arrogant. Suspicious. Elegant. Zealous. Wild. Insolent. Brawling. Crazy. Bold. Aloof. Flamboyant. Cynical. Manipulative. Opportunistic. Demagogic. Visionary. Ruthless. Vain. Fiery. Intolerant. Resentful. Wayward. Waspish. Charismatic. Venomous. Reckless. Theatrical. Added up, they describe a complex man.

In his flamboyance De Cosmos was the precursor of the most noteworthy premiers who followed him. In their unpredictable twists and turns they fitted the description of De Cosmos as a "political chameleon." There has been little fixed adherence to principles among B.C. premiers.

At the peak of the heated Confederation debate in 1870, De Cosmos declared that "political hatreds attest the vitality of a state." The maxim is debatable, but in keeping with his volatile style. The evidence is all around that British Columbia is enmeshed in political hatreds that do not allow good government.

Joe Martin

Chapter 3.

Fighting Joe

Amor De Cosmos was succeeded as premier by his Attorney-General, G.A. Walkem. Over the next twenty-five years there followed a succession of virtual nonentities in the office, nine in all. They left no legacy for the province other than political instability. The names Elliott, Beaven, Smithe, Davie, Turner, Semlin are barely remembered today, although they served in the province's highest office during a period of great expansion. Of the twenty-five men elected to the first Legislative Assembly, seven later became premier. Only Walkem served more than one term and the longest single administration was that of William Smithe, four years and two months.

Among this group, only John Robson stood out. A newspaperman like De Cosmos, he made a significant impact on the province during his long career as a journalist. His best years were behind him, however, when he became premier at the age of sixty-five in 1889. Even so, his three-year administration was one of the few that attempted popular reform, feeble as it may have been. Robson was a tired man and had lost some of the idealism of his early years as a crusading editor.

It was not until the turn of the century, February 28, 1900, to be exact, that some of De Cosmos' colour and flamboyance were restored to the Premier's Office in the person of Joseph "Fighting Joe" Martin. Martin's stay was brief, however. He was tossed out of office June 14 after three and a half turbulent months.

• • •

Unlike that of De Cosmos, Martin's early life is well documented. Joe was born in 1852 in the Ontario farming community of Milton. His father and his uncles were farmers, active and well-known in the little town. Joe's father rose to the position of mayor, but was disgraced for unknown reasons while Joe was still a boy. The family then moved across the border into Michigan.

The boy had never been close to his father, who became painfully introverted after his loss of prestige. The affair was traumatic for the son too. He became an embittered loner, a tendency exacerbated by a fall from a farm wagon that injured his leg. He was left with a permanent limp. Unable or unwilling to participate in youthful games, Joe turned to books and became a top student. After reading a biography of William Lyon Mackenzie, he tried to model himself on the great radical firebrand, defending the farmers against rapacious financiers and the monopolistic railway. The young Martin also idolized one of his teachers, and it was this attachment which first made him think of becoming a school teacher.

Although he had hated the railway company since it had bypassed Milton, his first job off the farm in Michigan was as a railroad telegrapher and dispatcher. During this period, while in his late teens, Joe toughened up by joining his workmates on visits to the bars and brothels of Detroit and learning the ways of the streets. Not long after his twentieth birthday, he enrolled at the Michigan State Normal School, but moved back to Canada the following year.

The Toronto Normal School, a bastion of conservatism and autocratic administration, could not long contain the boiling pot that was Joe Martin. After a series of escapades, he was expelled for what was described as "obstreperous behaviour." The exact details of his caper are unknown, but it may have resembled an incident described in Robert Barr's autobiographical novel, *The Measure of the Rule*. Barr, who attended the school at the same time as Martin, later portrayed his classmate as the belligerent "John Henceforth."

Barr pictured Henceforth as a coldly selfish man with a sneering disdain for his opponents, who were baited with sarcasm. "Something in his tone rouses virulent antagonism in the human race," Barr wrote. Henceforth's twisted mind was reflected in a crooked smile. He could never leave well enough alone. At the same time, Barr respected Henceforth-Martin's courage, which rose with the intensity of the threat against him. He became somewhat of a hero to his classmates by showing up the incompetence of the school's teachers and displaying a sort of nobility. He was respected and admired for his abilities, but never liked. Cold and distant, Henceforth was a friendless man.

After his ouster from the Toronto Normal School in May of 1874, Martin moved to Ottawa where he wrote the School Board exams and was granted a teaching certificate. For the next three years he taught at an Ottawa public school.

Martin became active in politics at this time, getting involved in local issues. He was particularly concerned about the growing enrolment at Catholic separate schools. This resentment grew into a bitter anti-French prejudice which would surface later with disastrous results for his political career. Always a man in a hurry, Martin had no time for prolonged debate or listening to the ideas of others. As soon as he had pronounced his opinion, Joe called for a vote on the issue under discussion.

In 1877, at the age of twenty-five, Martin enrolled at the University of Toronto. His first idea was to advance his teaching career, but being a school teacher was obviously too tame. Martin needed a field where his real talents would come into play, where the money was better and political ambitions could be more easily satisfied. The answer, of course, was law. He turned his attention to legal studies and passed the Ontario bar examinations. After marrying an Ottawa widow ten years his senior and with a young daughter, Martin decided to go west.

He settled in Portage la Prairie, Manitoba, where he opened an office and was admitted to the Manitoba Bar in 1882. With characteristic brashness, Martin immediately sought the Liberal nomination for an upcoming provincial general election. Not only was he successful in gaining the nomination, but he won the seat after a dispute over his polling-day tactics. As an Opposition back-bencher Martin quickly gained notoriety by criticizing the Speaker of the House. He was held in contempt of the Legislature until he had made an equivocal apology. In the words of a biographer Martin soon proved that he was "a powerful vote-getter, a forceful speaker and a shrewd manipulator of events." He made his mark in the House by arousing the bitter antagonism of his opponents.

Despite being accused of assault by a prominent Manitoba Tory, Martin was re-elected in 1886. Two years later, when the Conservative government was toppled, he became Attorney-General, Provincial Lands Commissioner, and Railway Commissioner in the new Liberal administration of Thomas Greenway.

Martin had always been an ardent supporter of the Liberals' free trade policies and now stepped up his fight against the tariffs of Sir John A. Macdonald. Martin favoured the free flow of goods to the U.S. and sought to break the stranglehold of the C.P.R. with a rail line from Winnipeg to St. Paul, Minnesota. But it was as Education Minister that he created the greatest stir.

Martin had been given the latter portfolio after a new Department of Education was created in 1890. Although not an Orangeman himself, Martin aligned himself with the anti-Catholic organization in its fight to end Manitoba's dual school system which catered to the significant French-Canadian population. The province was in an uproar, but Martin was instrumental in abolishing separate schools and French as an official language, arguing the case before the Supreme Court of

Canada and the Privy Council in London.

It was a generally popular move in the province, but antagonized Wilfrid Laurier and the federal Liberal party, represented in Manitoba by Clifford Sifton. With these powerful forces now aligned against him, Martin was under the gun and resigned from the Greenway government. He tried to win a federal seat but was defeated by the opposition of Sifton, who had taken over as Attorney-General.

After a brief return to his law practice, Martin decided in 1893, despite his differences with Laurier, to again seek a seat in the House of Commons in a byelection. This time he was successful and became the first Liberal from Winnipeg elected to the Commons. Three years later, however, he was defeated despite an overall Liberal victory when the CPR used its political clout and financial resources to oppose him. Martin had hopes of being taken into the cabinet through a Senate appointment or byelection, but was given a clear message when Laurier named Sifton as Minister of the Interior, the post Martin coveted.

Curiously, Martin then accepted a job as counsel for his old foe, the CPR. It was said that the lucrative position was set up with the company by his opponents, who wanted him out of the way. This belief gained credence when the CPR moved Joe to the end of the line at Vancouver.

Besides political controversy, Martin's fifteen-year stay in the Prairie province had been scarred by scandals. In 1890 the *Manitoba Free Press* accused Martin and his law partner, Smith Curtis, of rigging a number of land sales in a Portage la Prairie tax auction. And in the best Amor De Cosmos tradition, Martin also had a fistfight with another lawyer on a Portage la Prairie street. It was here that the sobriquet "Fighting Joe" was applied. Reinforced by subsequent battles, it stuck. A certain notoriety also attached itself to Martin in the town, with rumours about his private life.

The comparisons with De Cosmos are striking. One writer summed Martin up as "brilliant and erratic, of indomintable courage but disastrous judgement," a characterization applicable to both men. Both were also noted for the malevolence of the steely glare they fixed on opponents. The adjectives that have been applied to Martin are also similar in tone: Pugnacious. Impetuous. Magnetic. Boorish. Vindictive. Impulsive. Erratic. Temperamental. Blunt. Loud. Brainy. Domineering. Rash. Vain. Ambitious. Bellicose. Swashbuckling. Merciless. Vitriolic. Both men lived for and thrived on controversy.

In appearance, however, they could not have been more unlike. While De Cosmos was lean and pale with delicate features, Martin had a stocky build which tended to fat in later years. The most prominent feature of his small, round, balding head was a long, red, hooked nose. A tuft of scrubby, grey whiskers concealed a blotchy complexion and receding chin. With a rounded belly supported by skinny legs, his profile was described by a contemporary as that of a man who had swallowed a watermelon whole. Piercing, deepset black eyes under bushy brows and prominent beak accented a hawklike face. The cartoonists loved him.

• • •

Joe Martin blew into British Columbia like a winter storm. His reputation had preceded him and one newspaperman pleaded with Manitoba: "For God's sake, keep Martin and send on your blizzard." But Joe arrived in Vancouver in 1897 at the age of forty-five, accurately deducing that the mainland city had a more prosperous future than Victoria.

Martin soon became embroiled in a dispute with the Tory-dominated Law Society over a restriction requiring six months' residence before he could open a practice. A complaint that he had violated the rule was made to the Society by a Rossland lawyer, who also accused Smith Curtis of the same offence. Martin claimed that he and Curtis, who had moved to B.C. at about the same time, were merely business partners and were not practising law. A letter was produced, however, which had been sent out by Curtis to a client which represented himself and Martin as solicitors before the residency term had been completed.

Nevertheless, when Martin was called to the bar on October 14, 1897, he promptly wrote a heated letter to the Vancouver *Province* complaining that the Benchers were not acting in the public good but rather maintaining the legal profession as a "closed ring." The six-months' restriction prevented eminent lawyers from other provinces appearing as counsel in B.C. courts, he said. Martin argued that the power to disbar should be removed from the Benchers and placed with the courts, as in Manitoba. He had wasted no time in establishing himself as a legal maverick in his new locale.

Battler that he was, Martin could not have been dismayed to find that he already had a well-established opposition when he arrived. During his time as an MP in Ottawa he had made enemies in the Commons of both Edward G. Prior and Frank Barnard, both of whom had returned to become powers in provincial politics. The prominent Victoria lawyer and politician A.E. McPhillips had also been alienated by Martin in the Manitoba political frays before McPhillips moved west.

Politically, Martin could not have chosen a better time to arrive in the province. British Columbia's ever-turbulent politics were in an even more chaotic state than usual. It was a situation made for Martin's style and tactics, and he plunged in with gusto.

Despite the gibe of Price Ellison, the MLA for Yale, that he "had come into this province with all he possessed in a carpet bag," Martin was nominated in the four-seat Vancouver City riding in the July 9, 1898 provincial election and won on his first try. There were a number of irregularities and delayed countings in the election, including Martin's riding, and Joe revelled in the confusion of a political vacuum. He outraged many by issuing a press release from his office in the Hotel Vancouver with a proposed new cabinet roster headed by himself as Premier.

That was not yet to be, but the final results did spell the end of the undistinguished administration of Premier John H. Turner. Turner was reluctant to accept the verdict, however, and tried to hang on. But Lieutenant-Governor Thomas R. McInnes decided to intervene by refusing to sign cabinet orders-in-council. McInnes, who never regarded his position as merely ceremonial and later was disgraced for defying tradition, followed up with a curt letter dismissing Turner from office even though he had not been defeated in a Legislative vote.

McInnes turned first to former premier Robert Beaven,

who had just lost his seat in Victoria and was unable to round up enough supporters to form a government. Next to be approached was Charles Augustus Semlin, a wealthy rancher who was the last survivor of the first Legislative Assembly of 1871.

An unassuming man, Semlin had a difficult time forming a cabinet. He was forced to turn for help to the leaders of two rival factions, Francis Carter-Cotton and Joe Martin, who had already asserted himself into the forefront of provincial politics. Martin was named Attorney-General and Carter-Cotton Finance Minister. They quickly became bitter rivals, squabbling in public and making life miserable for Semlin. Carter-Cotton was reported to have made a secret deal with the CPR, which was still worried about its old nemesis Martin. Semlin later gave a huge land grant to a CPR subsidiary.

Martin added to Semlin's woes by scrapping with MLAs and the electorate. Encountering Price Ellison in the corridor after Ellison's carpet-bagger remark, Martin leaped at him yelling obscenities and had to be restrained.

Semlin managed to push through a number of reform measures during his brief tenure, including a reduction of the working day to eight hours. This, plus a bill designed to exclude further immigration of Asiatics, annoyed the mining community, which counted on the Orientals' cheap labour and long hours. Smith Curtis, who had set up a law practice in Rossland, invited his former partner to come up and pacify the influential Kootenay mine owners. Martin typically succeeded only in making matters worse. He appeared to have had a few drinks too many and when his audience became noisily restless during his rambling after-dinner speech, Joe's temper flared.

"I will not be silenced by hoboes in evening dress," he thundered. When the mining men retaliated by calling him a bum, Martin threatened to cut off a $35,000 government appropriation for a new courthouse in Rossland and rushed from the banquet room. He returned a short time later, probably at Curtis' prompting, to declare: "I wish to state that Rossland will get its $35,000 for a new courthouse, but you hoboes in evening dress can go to the devil."

When word of the fiasco got back to Victoria the *Colonist*

commented acidly that "Mr. Martin was certainly boorish in Rossland, but then, is he ever anything else?"

By now it was apparent to Semlin that Martin was the most troublesome member of his administration. The Premier asked his outspoken Attorney-General to resign for breaching cabinet solidarity. Joe balked and took his case to the caucus, demanding that Semlin himself step down. But the caucus, wary of this new whirlwind from the East, sided with the Premier and supported his ouster of Martin.

Semlin, meanwhile, knowing how vulnerable his administration was, avoided meeting the Legislature. Once again McInnes stepped boldly into the fray, ordering Semlin to call a session by October or hold an election. Semlin defied the Lieutenant-Governor, who appealed to Ottawa for support. McInnes was told to keep a lower profile. "Your ministers are at all times the proper judges of the time to call the Assembly," he was told by Secretary of State R.W. Scott. Privately, Scott was advising Laurier that McInnes "seems to have very crude notions of constitutional government." If he dismissed a second government without cause Ottawa might be forced to recall him, but since he had been appointed by the Liberals, "I presume it is desirable that he should be kept, if possible, from the commission of gross errors of judgement."

Eventually, however, Semlin could hold out no longer and the Legislature was called. There were a number of close votes before his inevitable defeat came in February of 1900 on a redistribution bill. Semlin desperately attempted to hang on by forming a new coalition, and seemed to have the tacit approval of McInnes in these efforts. Suddenly, however, McInnes changed course and summoned the Premier to Government House. There he charged Semlin with incompetence and financial irresponsibility, demanding his resignation. Semlin gave up under protest and the House voted by a margin of only twenty-two to fifteen to censure McInnes. Nothing ensued from the rebuke, however, except an addition to the growing list of black marks against the aggressive Lieutenant-Governor.

When McInnes then called upon Martin to form a new government, the House was outraged. It registered lack of confidence in Martin by a vote of twenty-eight to one. As the Lieutenant-Governor arrived to prorogue the session, the members rose in a body and left, chanting "We are the people, we are the people, and we must be obeyed." Price Ellison threw his hat in the air. McInnes proceeded to read his speech to the empty chamber, with only Martin and the Speaker in their seats and a crowded, hostile public gallery which hissed and jeered.

McInnes had tried to mollify Ottawa by claiming that Martin was the man "best able to meet the necessities of the situation, create decisive issues, and establish final order, and something like usual political conditions out of the chaos of factions into which provincial parties have been rent." The only thing wrong with that ringing endorsement was that Joe was much more adept at creating chaos than ending it.

● ● ●

It was an inauspicious beginning as premier for Martin, now regarded as a political pariah. He was taken aback by the open hostility of the legislators. None were willing to join his administration and he had a difficult time making up a cabinet. After taking on the portfolio of Attorney-General himself, he persuaded Smith Curtis, who was growing increasingly deaf, to leave his law practice in Rossland and come down to serve as Minister of Mines. A farmer from Agassiz, George Washington Beebe, was named Provincial Secretary. Corry S. Ryder, a grocery clerk, chatted with Martin during a train trip from Nanaimo to Victoria on the E & N Railway and after complimenting the new premier on his political acumen found himself Minister of Finance.

For the rest it was said that Joe roamed the streets of Victoria looking for suitable candidates. Someone described the cabinet as "a museum of political curiosities." Some, like the neophyte Ryder, did not last long. When Premier Martin sent a messenger to the Finance Department to summon Ryder to his office, the Minister sent back word that he was too busy. An enraged Martin dashed down the corridor to find Ryder busily signing cheques scattered all over his desk. Martin swept them on to the floor and told Ryder not to sign cheques in future before consulting him. Martin soon found a new Minister of Finance.

The next few months are unparalleled in the political history of the province, which is saying something in British Columbia, where the bizarre is often accepted as the norm. Martin could not risk calling the Legislature, where he faced certain defeat, and stalled off an election as long as possible. His pal, Lieutenant-Governor McInnes, who had been so tough with Turner and Semlin, looked the other way as Joe dodged and weaved. In Ottawa, Scott fumed.

Martin tried at first to consolidate his position by rallying the Liberal party to his support and bringing about the belated introduction of party politics to the province. But the Grits, many of whom had been previously bruised by the abrasive Martin, were too divided to unite behind the upstart Premier even if they had been so inclined. And Laurier continued to rebuff Joe in his bid for federal Liberal support.

So Martin attempted to win public backing through the tried-and-true British Columbia tactic of bashing Ottawa in the cause of provincial rights and more financial aid. Economic development at the time was keyed to the building of railways. Publicly Martin proposed that the government itself should construct and own the long-proposed line from the coast to the Kootenay mines. But behind the scenes he was negotiating with an old friend, James J. Hill, the flamboyant American railway promoter who wanted to expand his Great Northern Railroad from Spokane into the B.C. Interior and on to the coast. Hill had met Martin years earlier in Minnesota, when Joe was on a Manitoba delegation discussing free trade with prominent American businessmen. Hill, always on the lookout for Canadian friends in high places, had been impressed by the energetic Martin.

Hill is said to have given Martin $100,000 to fight the forthcoming election campaign, in exchange for a promise that he would get the Premier's support for his railway line in the province.

Eventually Martin called an election for June 10, 1900. It was a rough campaign. On April 26 a group called the Provincial Rights Association sent out a single sheet headed "Decree No.

37" which was "published for the information of the people." It denounced McInnes' "devious methods of government" and accused him of committing "a series of outrages against the province." Martin was described as a "hare-brained political conspirator." The screed concluded: "The people are asked to support men on whose records are written despotism, madness, tyranny, mis-government, misrepresentation, fraud, deception, demagognicism (sic). . . bigotry, usurpation and wrong. . .their political chicanery will be certain death to provincial credit and prosperity already on the verge of ruin."

The Nanaimo *Herald* called Martin "the Lucifer of provincial politics." The *Colonist* said Martin's brief administration had been "a political farce which had brought this glorious province into disrepute." British Columbia was the butt of "the scorn and contempt of the intelligent world." It was true that, not for the last time, the rest of Canada concluded that British Columbia had gone politically mad. Even the U.S. took note of the unruly state of affairs to the north. The San Francisco *Post* commented: "The standard of American politics is usually regarded by our Canadian friends as at a disgracefully low level — but it would be difficult indeed to find in the whole of the United States a politician whose public speeches are punctuated by so many profane adjectives as that which the Hon. J. Martin of British Columbia is credited with."

On June 2 Secretary of State Scott wrote McInnes: "Not a single member of the existing Government had then (Feb. 28, when Martin took office) or even has up to the present time received the approval of the people. Only one of them had ever been a member of the Legislature, and he had no following; and I think it is without any parallel in the history of responsible government that a body of men, five-sixths of whom had never been members of the Legislature, should be permitted to carry on a Government for three months without public sanction or approval."

And the public was not about to give its approval. Despite a feisty, belligerent campaign against great odds, Martin was repudiated by the electorate. No members of his jerry-built cabinet were elected and only six of his supporters made it. Another seven MLAs were regarded as half-hearted supporters, but since the remainder of the thirty-eight elected members were solidly opposed to him, Martin had no hope of carrying on. The electorate failed, however, to provide an alternative. Charles Semlin and his forces were obliterated and, in the words of one observer, "the vast majority of the members-elect recognized no leader and adhered to no policy except self-interest."

Before resigning, Martin advised McInnes that the only possible choice for premier appeared to be James Dunsmuir, the wealthy scion of the coal-mining and railway baron, Robert Dunsmuir. This choice was widely regarded as an interim solution to the province's problems. Dunsmuir had been a member of the Legislature for two years but had no real interest in politics. He did not relish the cut and thrust of debate and accepted the post only out of a sense of duty.

Along with a new premier, the province also got a new Lieutenant-Governor. After Martin's resignation Laurier decided the time had come to end the stormy tenure of Thomas McInnes. Although McInnes had been widely criticized for his dismissal of Premiers Turner and Semlin, it was his choice of Martin that upset Ottawa most. Joe was still regarded there with a mixture of fear and loathing. He had never minced words in his criticism of federal policy toward western Canada and his assertion of provincial rights. The corporate sector, which provided financial backing for whichever party was in power federally, also distrusted Martin and wasted no time in pressing Laurier to oust Joe's ally McInnes.

McInnes himself was distrusted by both parties in Ottawa. He had begun his political career as a Tory supporter of John A. Macdonald, serving in the Commons from 1878 to 1882, when he was elevated to the Senate. McInnes had been investing heavily in real estate at Port Moody in the expectation that it would become the railroad terminus. McInnes bitterly broke with Macdonald when it was decided to extend the line to Vancouver, costing him thousands. When Laurier rebuffed his bid for a cabinet seat, McInnes moved to Victoria in 1890 and began to actively campaign for the post of Lieutenant-Governor. He believed in that post "he could more effectively fulfil his destiny as the saviour of the province than as a Senator,'' as historian John Saywell put it.

Laurier found it expedient to accede to McInnes' wishes in 1897 when the Prime Minister needed a Senate opening for a more reliable Liberal. A vain man who loved the meddling and intrigue of politics, McInnes was soon bored by his ceremonial post and began to take the active role in British Columbia politics which eventually led to his downfall. He had found an ally in Martin. Both men resented the Eastern bias of the Laurier-Sifton administration and both hated the CPR with a passion.

The Prime Minister advised McInnes on June 19 that he should resign. McInnes refused and Laurier was forced to remove him by an order-in-council dated June 21 which declared that his ''official conduct has been subversive of the principles of responsible government.'' Only one Lieutenant-Governor in Canada had previously been removed from office — precipitated by a political row in Quebec in 1878 — and none has been ousted since.

• • •

Martin's defeat after only 106 days in office — the shortest tenure in British Columbia history — was just another setback in a long and stormy career. However, he still had a role to play in the provincial Legislature before moving on to other political stages.

Nominally, Martin was now the opposition leader in the House, but this was an amorphous position in the absence of political parties, and he in fact did all that he could to prop up the tottering Dunsmuir administration. Since he clearly had no chance of returning to a position of leadership in the province, there was no incentive to bring down the government as there had been before.

But Martin, unhappy unless he was in some kind of scrap, found a new opponent in a formidable new figure who had made his entrance on the political stage quietly at the age of twenty-eight in 1898: Richard McBride. A lawyer who specialized in mining litigation, McBride was inconspicuous during the brief Martin-McInnes era. With his charming wife Mary, the affable McBride seemed more interested at that time in Victoria's social life than its political controversies and moved in the same circles as the Dunsmuirs.

It was not surprising when Premier Dunsmuir picked the bright young newcomer to become Minister of Mines, but McBride now fixed his eye on bigger prizes. He soon resigned and crossed the floor, ostensibly because Dunsmuir had named a former Martin appointee to his cabinet. On the eve of the 1902 session McBride was elected leader of the disparate group in opposition to the Dunsmuir administration. This did not sit well with Martin, who had nominally held that position despite the fact he had done little opposing.

When he entered the House just before the opening prayer, Martin saw that he had been moved down the front row and a chair with McBride's name placed where he had been. Joe protested loudly but was interrupted when the Speaker called the House to order and the chaplain entered. Martin walked scowling to his assigned seat, but did not remain. As the MLAs stood with heads bowed in prayer, Joe slipped along behind the row of desks until he was standing near the chair of McBride, who did not see him. Just as the closing 'Amen' was being intoned, Joe plunked himself down in the new Opposition Leader's chair.

A scuffle ensued in which Smith Curtis, now bitterly estranged from his former partner, grabbed Martin by the neck and tried to pull him out of the chair. Smith Curtis was helped by two of McBride's friends, but they in turn were grabbed by two Martin supporters. Joe simply grasped the arms of the chair more firmly and planted his feet on the floor. Shocked at first, the public galleries were soon amused by the antics below. The Speaker called for order and threatened to clear the galleries, but to no avail. It was just like the old days of De Cosmos when the Legislative chamber often resembled a Roman circus.

After the pushing and shoving stopped, there was a brief debate in which it was agreed that the seating plan would be restored to that of the last session. Joe had won the day, and McBride was forced to bide his time.

While Martin continued to prop up the inept Dunsmuir government as nominal leader of the opposition, McBride hammered away at the beleaguered Premier. At the same time both

Martin and McBride were trying to bolster their positions through party allegiancies. Martin succeeded in taking over the provincial Liberal party, but lacked real clout because he was still vigorously opposed by the federal Grits. McBride attempted to take over the provincial Conservatives, but was defeated by the party's old guard led by former federal cabinet minister E. G. Prior.

, When Dunsmuir resigned in frustration in November, 1902, it was Prior who was invited to form a new government. He fared little better than Martin, and was forced out of office by the following June. In that brief period three of his cabinet ministers resigned in the fall-out from a scandal in which two of them were revealed to have been in collusion with a group of railway financiers. Then Prior himself lost all credibility when a Legislative committee found he had ordered that a substantial government contract be given to his own hardware and machinery business. When Prior refused to resign, the new Lieutenant-Governor, Sir Henri Joly de Lotbiniere, dismissed him. It was the third time in the province's short history that such action had been taken. Only Quebec, with two, has had similar ousters. Prior's removal from office was the last in B.C. and the province then entered a period of relative stability under Premier Richard McBride.

• • •

Martin, meanwhile, was ready to give up on the province. He had devoted a lot to politics, including his body. In 1903 while convalescing after treatment for his gimpy leg, a provincial general election was called. Martin promptly went to his doctor and asked to have the leg amputated just below the knee. The doctors believed they could have saved the leg, but Joe insisted on the operation so that he could get on with the campaign in Vancouver. Despite such heroic efforts, Martin was rejected by the voters.

He had tried to get appointed to the Bench, but was blackballed by his Ottawa enemies and reluctantly returned to his law practice in Vancouver. He was counsel for the City of Vancouver in 1905 and chief solicitor for James J. Hill's Great Northern Railway the following year. That was the least Hill could do for his old ally after swiftly cutting off his political funding when Martin lost power in the House. Joe demanded large fees and was able to accumulate substantial blocks of property in Vancouver at this time. He also enjoyed playing high-stakes stud poker at the Vancouver Club.

Not all his legal work was prestigious. He also took on the case of Desiree Brothier, a notorious Vancouver madam charged with keeping a brothel. Her account book, containing names of numerous leading citizens, was whisked away by Joe during the trial. The judge issued a search warrant for it but Martin persuaded him to keep the contents confidential so as not to embarrass some of the city's prominent businessmen and politicians. It was a precedent to be followed in later, similar cases and is now a well-established B.C. tradition.

Despite his discouragements and frustrations in the political arena, or perhaps because of them, Martin's pugnaciousness never diminished. At a meeting of the B.C. Liberal Association in the Hotel Vancouver he exchanged blows with the Association president, lawyer Lyman Duff of Victoria, a future Chief Justice of the Supreme Court of Canada. The fracas started when Duff made a jocular remark, Martin called him a liar, Duff hit first, and Martin responded. Friends intervened to separate the combatants.

Martin was involved in another altercation when he tried to pass through a roped-off area to gain access to the CPR dock in Vancouver. A railway constable moved to stop him and Joe answered with a stiff right to the jaw. The battle continued until two more constables arrived to rescue their colleague, who was getting the worst of it. Charges were contemplated but not pressed against Martin, so he launched an unsuccessful civil action for assault against his old foe and onetime client, the CPR.

In 1908 the Asiatic Exclusion League nominated Martin as its candidate in the general federal election. The League's platform called for formation of an Independent Western Party for the four western provinces. It also favoured exclusion of Chinese, Japanese, Hindus ''and all other undesirable foreigners.'' Abolition of the Senate and resistance to any change in the BNA Act which would force separate schools on B.C. were other platform planks. They made little impression on the electorate and Martin failed to get enough votes to save his deposit.

• • •

At age fifty-seven, it was time for another move. Martin had been fascinated with British politics since a visit there during his days as Manitoba attorney-general to argue the separate schools case before the Privy Council. The great Liberal reformer William Gladstone was one of his heroes. And just as De Cosmos had found a Canadian to idolize in Joseph Howe, so did Martin with Edward Blake. Blake had become a British MP after his distinguished political career in Ontario. It was not surprising then that Martin turned up in Britain early in 1909 and three months later was running as a Liberal candidate in Stratford. He lost, but within a year tried again in the London riding of St. Pancras-East and won.

The British did not quite know what to make of this brawler from the colonies. "Mr. Martin is a burly man with something of the air of a prosperous farmer," said the *Daily Mail*. "His style is big and bold and his eloquence runs like a river in flood. He has fought thirteen elections in Canada and lost four." The latter comment was apt in making him sound like the middle-rank political prizefighter he undoubtedly was.

Nevertheless, his victory in Britain meant Joe had served in four separate senior elected bodies in two countries, an unmatched record.

Martin's approach to politics didn't change merely because he was now in a more civilized environment than the British Columbia Legislature. As before, he tried to bowl over anyone who got in his way. Martin urged that Rudyard Kipling be prosecuted for sedition following publication of his poem "Ulster" denouncing Home Rule for Ireland, a cause to which Martin (and Edward Blake) was passionately devoted. He apparently regarded it as similar to the provincial rights issue back home. As well as home rule, he also spoke in favour of abolishing the House of Lords and the award of titles to Canadians, an obvious dig at the knighthood conferred on Richard McBride.

Martin also wanted the British government to censure Governor-General Earl Grey for making public speeches opposing the policy of reciprocity with the U.S. being pushed by Laurier.

Another cause which Martin had first taken up in Canada — giving the vote to women — was continued in Britain, and he even attended a Suffragette rally. The unpopularity of this crusade was pointed up by a B.C. journal which described those participating in the event as "reckless creatures . . . an unruly crowd of screaming, biting, punching, kicking, hair-pulling, militant" women who had the nerve to call themselves ladies.

Joe made a visit back to Vancouver while still a British MP — the Vancouver *News-Advertiser* called it a "meteoric appearance" — and demonstrated that Britain hadn't taken off the rough edges. He lashed out at practically everybody. Politics in Canada were rotten, Martin said, as if just discovering the fact. His special target was Laurier, who had lost the general election of 1911. Martin arrived in the midst of a federal investigation into immigration and opium smuggling irregularities and jumped right in as if he had never left. Historian James Morton has remarked that he "did not add anything specific to the investigation, but he certainly enlivened the proceedings."

Joe continued to drift back and forth across the Atlantic. He was in Vancouver when war broke out in 1914 and, instead of attempting to return, reopened his law office and became a candidate for mayor of the city while still a British MP. Vancouver voters turned their backs on him. They were unimpressed by his campaign promise to cut the salaries of the mayor and aldermen and clean out the "dead wood" from City Hall. He also attacked the previous council for turning over the False Creek flats to the CNR for a song. When he tried again the following year, Martin suffered another defeat. Despite being elected to two Houses of Commons and two provincial Legislatures, he never made it into the mayor's chair. He started a newspaper in Vancouver in 1915, the *Evening Journal*, which he hoped would help him get elected. It lasted only three months despite his lively editorials.

At age sixty-two Martin had lost none of his belligerence. While defending an accused counterfeiter, Martin squared off in the courtroom with Deputy Police Chief J. MacRae. The two men continued fighting in the corridor after being ejected by Magistrate Augustus Shaw.

After these setbacks in his former bailiwick, Martin returned to Britain and took his seat in the Commons again. Three months later, however, he suddenly resigned his St. Pancras seat and came back home to stay, declaring his intention to run federally for the Liberals in Cariboo in the next general election.

But Martin's behaviour was becoming increasingly erratic. He changed his mind once more and in 1917 went back to London, turning his back on a nomination he had received in the Kootenays. In England he said he intended to stay this time and joined the Labour Party. He had long since fouled his relations with the Liberals by denouncing both Asquith and Lloyd George, apparently because they had ignored his political talents. (He also crossed swords with a budding young politician named Winston Churchill).

Joe's final journey home was made in 1919. He returned to the law and practised for a time with the flamboyant Gerry McGeer. He ran as an independent in all the general elections that came along, but gathered few votes. Once despised and feared in political circles, now he was simply forgotten — an irrelevant, pathetic figure somewhat like Amor De Cosmos in his latter days.

Martin preserved his sanity to the end, but his intellectual powers waned rapidly. He died, aged seventy-one, on March 2, 1923, of diabetes after being the first person treated in Vancouver with the new drug insulin. He left most of his $100,000 estate to a Mrs. Emily Cakebread, a housekeeper. There was no scandal attached to the will; his wife Eliza had died in 1914 and there were no surviving children. There was litigation, however, as distant relatives contested the will in a lawsuit that dragged on for fourteen years. In a final ironic twist to Martin's bedevilled career, the judgement was not handed down until the depths of the Depression when his properties were practically worthless and there was not enough left in the estate to cover legal costs.

Martin's career is best summed up by Robert Barr in *The Measure of the Rule*. John Henceforth, Barr wrote, had scored political victories "over obstacles that appeared insurmountable, only to be crushed later by his colleagues . . . unsuccessful but undismayed, he has moved from place to place, rapidly becoming the leading man in each locality where he stationed himself, filling with alarm the party to which he is opposed.'' He lacked ''some one ingredient in his nature which would have made him a hero of the world.''

Richard McBride

Chapter 4.

Sir Richard

Richard McBride's arrival in the premier's chair marked a significant change in the nature of the office. British Columbia's destiny now moved from the hands of 19th century eccentrics and individualists into those of the smooth-tongued wheeler-dealers. Fistfights were out; glibness was in. The economic policies of resource exploitation were basically the same, but now the urbanity of the boardroom covered up much of what was once out in the open. Public relations men and image-makers still lay in the future, but the tone was set.

McBride, in fact, did not need outside help to bamboozle the public. He was a natural, the golden boy of B.C. politics. There has never been another like him until handsome, vain Bill Vander Zalm took office some eighty years later. These two men had more in common than good looks. Both were showmen blessed with the gift of the gab, serving up frothy speeches to receptive audiences. (Vander Zalm found the cynical, informed voters of the 1980s a much harder sell, however).

McBride had an easy time with an electorate much like the one W.A.C. Bennett would later enjoy, an electorate eager to hear the good word from a man of boundless optimism and good cheer. As with Bennett, he was the right man at the right time in a period of booming expansion. (Bennett was anything but glamorous in appearance and lacked the charm of McBride and Vander Zalm, but he was more than their match in boldness of vision, energy, enthusiasm and malarkey).

McBride's geniality and charm were legendary. Wandering into a Fraser Valley dairy cattle show and asked to speak, he asked a local party official what he should talk about. Told of plans to start a canned milk factory in the district, McBride launched into a spontaneous speech, which he titled "From the Teat to the Tin," expounding on the benefits which would accrue to the farmers from such a project. His audience lapped it up.

The one characteristic McBride shared with most other premiers was the lack of a political doctrine. He was a pragmatic conservative with a keen instinct for seizing the right opportunities. It was said that he was a follower of the 11th Commandment: "Thou shall not be found out." Expediency and political trickery were his stock-in-trade. Like Bennett, he regarded politics as war and elections as coups.

● ● ●

Richard McBride was the first native-born premier. (There have been only four since — Simon Fraser Tolmie, Byron Johnson, Dave Barrett and Bill Bennett). He was born in New Westminster on December 15, 1870, the offspring of a most unusual union: his mother was a convent-reared Catholic and his father an Orangeman. Arthur Hill McBride, an Ulsterman, had met and married Irish-born Mary D'Arcy in California before moving north to B.C. He became a policeman in New Westminster, moving up the constabulary ladder until he was warden of the federal penitentiary.

Richard graduated from Dalhousie Law School and was called to the bar in New Westminster in 1892, joining a firm with good Conservative connections. With an eye already fixed on a political career, he looked for ways of making money in a hurry. He decided on the bustling mining community of Atlin in the far north of the province, where in claims dispute litigation he soon amassed a $4,000 stake for his first plunge into public life.

Returning to New Westminster, the twenty-six-year-old McBride captured the Conservative nomination for the federal general election of July, 1896. His platform shamelessly appealed to the bigotry of his constituents by calling for a ban on employment of Chinese and Japanese in the Fraser River salmon canneries. He also said only British subjects should be allowed to fish. But McBride was crushed in the Laurier landslide despite his opportunism.

Undaunted, McBride was back on the hustings two years later, seeking a provincial seat in nearby Dewdney riding. This time he was successful and within another two years was a cabinet minister under James Dunsmuir.

Despite his social connections with the Dunsmuirs, McBride did not feel any obligation of political loyalty. Knowing Dunsmuir was no politician and that his days as Premier were numbered, McBride wanted to be in a position to take over when the inevitable day came. Biding his time, he found an opportunity when Dunsmuir appointed as Provincial Secretary a former member of the Martin administration, J.C. Brown. McBride promptly resigned with a self-righteous flourish and moved into opposition. (An equally ambitious W.A.C. Bennett mimicked his course years later). McBride picked up a few other defectors along the way. More important, he also gained the invaluable support and financial help of the CPR. The *Colonist* observed that "Mr. McBride is strongly impressed with the fact that he is destined to be party leader" and had been waiting his chance to make a break.

McBride tried in 1902 to take over leadership of the provincial Conservative party, but lost out to the Old Guard forces led by E.G. Prior. When Dunsmuir resigned in November of that year McBride watched in frustration as Prior took over as premier. But Prior's administration lasted only a little longer than that of Joe Martin and finally, on June 1, 1903, Richard McBride began a twelve-year reign, by far the longest in the province to that time and second only to W.A.C. Bennett's unbreakable record of twenty-one years. He was only thirty-two, the youngest premier in the country and in the history of B.C.

One day after taking office McBride announced in the House that his government would be formed on strict party lines for the first time in the province. This meant dumping some of his former Liberal colleagues in opposition, causing bitterness among those who had expected to be invited into his administration. One of these, Charles W. Munro, is said to have told McBride: "There is one difference between you and Judas, Dick. Judas had the decency to go out and hang himself."

But McBride, the sixth premier in a turbulent five-year period, knew that the electorate — and potential investors — craved a stability which he believed could only be achieved through party discipline and continuity. An election was called for October and after campaigning for more money from Ottawa and control of Oriental immigration, McBride won his political gamble, but just barely. The Tories gained a slim majority with twenty-one seats, against seventeen Liberals and two Socialists. After appointing a Speaker, the Premier held only one more than the combined opposition. But it was a situation made for McBride, a chance to employ his considerable political skills.

• • •

With his meteoric rise to the highest office in the province, Richard McBride was not shackled by the cautiousness of experience. He had skipped over the drudgery and discipline of political office and was willing to try anything, to fly where others merely walked.

His natural gifts gave McBride the confidence to believe he could accomplish anything he attempted. It seemed to his opponents that he had been over-endowed with charm in the cradle. The winsome baby grew into the handsome man, six feet tall with flowing wavy hair which was nicely flecked with grey before he was thirty. He seemed always to be flashing a warm, magnetic smile. Little wonder he came to be known as "The Plumed Knight."

On the more practical side he was gifted with wit and fluency from his Irish ancestry. Urbane and voluble, he exuded good humour and cheer. He loved crowds and adulation and had a remarkable memory for names and faces.

In the Legislature these skills were turned blindingly on the two Socialists he needed to ensure the survival of his government. The unfortunate pair, James H. Hawthornwaite of Nanaimo and Parker Williams of Newcastle, representing the exploited and militant coal miners, were charmed right out of their reforming idealism. McBride threw them a few crumbs, but not enough to upset the financial interests. His main goal was to straighten out the province's chaotic finances and restore confidence in the money houses. B.C.'s credit rating was disastrously low.

McBride's lack of concern for the working people was demonstrated when a delegation of families from Nanaimo approached him to seek the release of coal miners who had been imprisoned for going out on an illegal strike. The petitioners got no support from the Premier, who told them that only Ottawa could grant clemency in such cases. He refused to endorse their plea to the Dominion Government and brushed off the threat of a general strike in support of the miners.

To build up a strong Conservative party organization for the next election McBride needed to distribute some patronage projects, but found himself short of funds. The solution was obvious: sell off the province's lands, rich in timber and minerals. When word went out of the government's intention, syndicates were quickly formed to take advantage of the bargains, grabbing large chunks of land at bargain-basement prices. The main industry of British Columbia became real estate. The speculators had a field day.

There was irony in the fact that McBride was following the economic development policies spelled out by Joe Martin, who never had the chance to implement them. And so McBride became the first in a line of 20th century B.C. premiers to give away the farm. Inheriting a resource-rich province coveted by outsiders, they could not resist the lure of investment to spur expansion and growth while filling the Treasury. The fact that the profits were funnelled outside the province did not concern them as long as the voters were caught up in the fever.

The province's sudden prosperity lured thousands of immigrants. As the population soared, a land rush replaced the gold rush. But the newcomers settled at their own risk. When they asked the government for maps they were given CPR promotional folders. And as one critic noted, "If a man wants land for farming in B.C., he must either pay a fancy price for it from speculators, or he must choose at his own risk a piece of land, clear it, cultivate, build his home on it, and all on the chance that at the end of a year, or two years, or three, he would be told that the land had been claimed by another man — probably somebody's political friend — and that he is a trespasser." The only way to ensure security was to become an open and ardent supporter of the McBride government.

Railway mania had subsided somewhat by the time McBride became premier, the inevitable result of the scandals of previous regimes. But the premier laid the groundwork for what would become his dominant policy — and consequent downfall — by turning over land to the railroad developers. Ten thousand acres on Kaien Island near the mouth of the Skeena River was sold for $1 an acre to the Grand Trunk Pacific for its terminus, and 860,000 acres was granted to a CPR land-holding subsidiary. The CPR showed its gratitude in the next election campaign by liberally supplying McBride with funds, free railway cars for barnstorming the province, as well as complimentary telegraph service.

By the time McBride was ready to call for a new mandate in February of 1907, he was an immensely popular figure around the province. Prosperity was in the air and labour was at peace. Any problems were blamed on Ottawa. Bowing to the pressure of business supporters who wanted cheap labour, the Dominion Government had allowed an increase in Oriental immigration, a move which was not well-received by the populace of B.C. McBride capitalized on this discontent by establishing himself as the "champion of white British Columbia."

He went to Ottawa to complain that British Columbia had

paid $19 million more to the Dominion Government since joining Confederation than it had received. Though the numbers would change, that was to become a familiar rallying cry for years to come. McBride warned that if he didn't get what he wanted from the feds, in full, he would go to Westminster, "the heart of the Empire," for redress. Some newspapers talked of secession. Western alienation was stirring again.

Just before the campaign began, two of McBride's senior cabinet ministers resigned under the clouds of separate scandals; Tory stalwart Charles H. Tupper broke with the government over a number of issues; and taxes were high, but the voters didn't seem to mind any of this. They gave McBride a comfortable majority of twenty-seven to fifteen in the new House.

Some of the voters might have been influenced by a front-page story in the Vancouver *Province* a few days before the election which declared that the Grand Trunk Pacific and the Dominion Government planned to import 50,000 Japanese to work on the railroad. It was not the last time the *Province* would attempt to influence an election with scare tactics.

• • •

McBride was an ardent Anglophile and Anglo-Canadian solidarity was a life-long cause. In 1901 he was a founding member of the British Empire League, an association to promote the Empire and its role in world. In a speech to the Canadian Manufacturers Association in 1910 McBride declared: "We British Columbians are good Canadians, but we are still more, intense Britishers."

It was not surprising, then, that the Premier visited England soon after his 1907 victory. His vanity fed on flattery; McBride strutted like a peacock in the warmth of his reception by London's bankers and financiers. Encouraged by his enthusiastic invitations, they saw new opportunities for profit in the most faraway province of the Canadian colony. His ardent imperialism made many friends in England, including the young Winston Churchill, Under-Secretary of State for Colonial Affairs.

At home the burning issue continued to be Oriental

immigration to meet the demand for cheap labour by lumbermen and railway contractors. A total of 11,000 Japanese came into the province in 1906 and 1907. Asiatics numbered one in every ten men in the Vancouver area. Tensions ran high. Ottawa seemed unconcerned with the problem, supporting the British policy of expanding trade with the Orient and permitting large-scale immigration, which affected only the West Coast. Persistent attempts by B.C. to introduce discriminatory legislation were repeatedly vetoed by the Dominion Government. McBride's foes accused him of exploiting anti-Asian sentiment by supporting the exclusion legislation, even though he knew it had no chance of being allowed. The new Lieutenant-Governor, former premier James Dunsmuir, the largest employer of Orientals in the province, was accused of a conflict of interest when he refused to sign one of the bills after Ottawa had killed five earlier ones. One historian has concluded that in his manipulation of this issue McBride "never cleared himself of the charge that he had acted improperly and deceptively."

It *was* a difficult matter for McBride, however. Another observer has written: "As an ardent Imperialist and at the same time a loyal British Columbian, he found himself torn between his desire to conform in every way with Imperial policy, and the need to protect the special interests of his province."

But McBride had a diversion for yet another election campaign after just two years: a grand new railway plan, a grid that would extend new tracks into the four corners of the province. The time seemed ripe. The economy was generally buoyant and the Treasury was brimming, enough to guarantee millions of dollars of bonds for Canadian Northern promoters William Mackenzie and Donald Mann to bring a second transcontinental line into the province. Once again the cabinet was divided on the wisdom of McBride's ambitious scheme, but he knew he had the people with him. He was right. They gave him thirty-eight of forty-two seats.

The Opposition was made up of two Liberals and two Socialists. One of the latter, however, was later repudiated by his militant Nanaimo constituents after it was discovered he had been caught up in the economic fever and was an ardent land speculator. Then one of the Liberals defected to the Tories and with just two opposition members left, House rules eliminated the need for time-consuming roll-call votes. Important railway legislation was whistled through. The legislature had become a mere rubber stamp for the government.

McBride meanwhile traipsed off once again to New York and London to taste the fruits of victory and woo more capitalists to his domain. British Columbia, he told them, was an "Empire in embryo." And McBride was the undisputed Emperor, at the peak of his power. Finance Minister Robert Tatlow and Lands Minister F.J. Fulton did not have the confidence McBride and his principal supporters gave Mann and Mackenzie, and both had resigned before the election. But Attorney-General William J. Bowser, Provincial Secretary H. Esson Young and the new finance minister, Price Ellison, all shared McBride's expansionist dreams and now there was no-one in cabinet to sound a note of caution.

McBride's continued success at the polls gave him a new status in the national Conservative party. After ten years as Opposition Leader, Robert Borden was discouraged and wanted to retire. In early 1911 he offered McBride the job, confident that the party would accept him. McBride must have been tempted to step onto the larger stage, but was warned bluntly by Bowser of the risks involved. At that time Laurier seemed unbeatable. McBride declined. Few could guess that Borden would turn things around within the year, becoming prime minister January 1, 1912.

Borden had asked McBride to run in the election, but he restricted himself to participating in the campaign, fighting reciprocity by lambasting the Americans and waving the Union Jack. (One of his concerns about trade reciprocity with the Americans was that increased north-south trade would adversely affect his railway projects).

The Tories took all seven seats in B.C. and McBride was offered a cabinet post, which he declined. It was the last time he would be wooed by Ottawa. McBride had assumed that his province would receive a better financial deal from Ottawa when the Conservatives finally succeeded in ousting Laurier, but Borden conceded little. A few years later, when he was looking for an honourable escape from B.C. politics, McBride made overtures for a Senate seat or the prestigious post of Canadian High Commissioner in Britain, but neither materialized. He settled for the comparatively lowly post of B.C. Agent-General in London.

● ● ●

Borden had succeeded with hard political work, something McBride was finding increasingly distasteful. He much preferred dining with the nobs at London's Savoy Hotel than tending the grassroots. More and more he left the work of government in Bowser's tough hands.

McBride went to Britain in June of 1911 to attend the Coronation of George V and the accompanying gala celebrations. It was a grand time. On his return he decided it would be opportune to consolidate his position with yet another election — his fourth in nine years. Until 1915 governments were required to hold elections every four years instead of the present five, but McBride never waited beyond three years. Similar tactics were followed by W.A.C. Bennett in his record-breaking term when he called five elections in his first eleven years in office. When the ballots were counted after the March 12, 1912, vote the opposition had been obliterated. McBride won forty seats, with the other two going to the Nanaimo-area Socialists.

During another jaunt to Britain two months later McBride was granted a long personal interview with the new monarch. On his return Borden recommended to the Governor-General that McBride be granted a knighthood. In September of 1912, at the age of forty-two, he was invested with the Order of Knight Commander of St. Michael and St. George. To most British Columbians the elegant Sir Richard became the symbol of their new prosperity. But some who looked more closely noted that the man once known as "The People's Dick" now tended to put on more airs. He was no longer one of the boys. There were many factors leading to his downfall, but the boost knighthood gave to his already over-weening pride played no small part.

There were a few small warning signs of economic troubles to come, such as pockets of unemployment, labour unrest and Okanagan fruit-growers going bankrupt, but for the first six months of 1912 nobody paid attention. They were all too busy riding the crest of the boom and reaping huge profits. Many were outsiders, lured to the province by McBride's exuberant sales pitches on his tours abroad. Some, especially the friends he had made in London, seemed to be privy to inside information on government plans. Soon after one of his visits to England, two wealthy British parliamentarians bought 12,000 acres of prime Okanagan fruit land. American investors, including such powerful interests as the Rockefellers, were more interested in the government-held timber lands being put up for grabs. Large amounts of European capital went into real estate. Ordinary town-lots in Prince George were selling for as much as $10,000 and Kamloops was advertised as the future "Los Angeles of Canada."

The government's mania for railways continued unabated. In January of 1912 six major railway bills sped through the House in four days. The Kettle Valley Company, a CPR subsidiary, was promised aid of $10,000 a mile for a fifty-mile extension. The CPR got $100,000 for a line linking Kaslo and Slocan. But the biggest plum was saved for the promoters of the new Pacific and Great Eastern Railroad to run 450 miles from Vancouver to connect with the Grand Trunk Pacific at Prince George and eventually carry on northward to the Peace River and who knew how far, perhaps Alaska and the Arctic Circle.

McBride's handling of the PGE contract can only be described as curious. A number of large railroad syndicates, including American and British consortiums, wanted to build and operate the line. Although they were experienced and well-financed, McBride turned to Foley, Welch and Stewart, a firm which had operated only as railway contractors. Jack W. Stewart, one of the principals, was a high-profile Liberal supporter who had helped found the Vancouver *Sun* to give the party a voice in provincial affairs. On top of all that, the law firm of Attorney-General Bowser, who worked out details of the PGE agreement, represented Foley, Welch and Stewart.

The contracting firm was able to conclude the deal only by

having the government guarantee its construction bonds to a limit of $35,000 a mile. Income from the sale of the bonds would be held in a trust fund to be transferred to the company by the Minister of Finance as construction proceeded. Other benefits granted by the government included generous chunks of land and exemption from taxation until 1926. For its part, the company agreed not to apply for any federal assistance. That meant Ottawa would have no control over what would be a strictly provincial railway, something McBride keenly desired. He had been frustrated by the Dominion Government on more than one occasion in his attempts to gain concessions from the Canadian Northern and Grand Trunk Pacific railways.

There was no mention of Asiatic labour in the contract between the government and the PGE, however McBride later confirmed that the company agreed "that they shall employ no yellow men." He added that "Asiatics are absolutely excluded from all public work in British Columbia."

The most dubious aspect of the whole affair was the awarding of the building contracts. In September, 1912, with financing assured, the board of directors, instead of calling for tenders, signed an agreement with one of the partners, Patrick Welch, to construct the line. Welch dutifully resigned as vice-president of the Pacific Great Eastern, but there was little doubt that he, Stewart and Timothy Foley would be splitting the profits, which promised to be handsome.

Just as the PGE construction got underway, however, the economic boom began to crumble. Credit suddenly tightened up. Everything was up for sale but there were no buyers. The demand for metals dropped sharply and Kootenay mining towns like Sandon were going broke. Provincial revenues plummeted. McBride's money-raising forays to London didn't look so good now. British financiers, on whom he had depended for funding provincial expansion, were alarmed by political developments in Europe and the threat of war and cut off the money supply to enterprises abroad. McBride tried desperately to offset this loss by talking about extending the PGE to Alaska and Tacoma to get the Americans interested, but to no avail.

The Premier's response to the growing crisis was to act as

if it didn't exist. In the legislature he carried on with his amiable manner and benign smile after using "sweet-oil" tactics on the caucus. But "in days of adversity," one observer commented, "his charm seemed less engaging." Instead of starting to retrench, "he borrowed heavily, talked confidently and hung on grimly," in the words of one critic. The government refused to cut spending on public works, except for the proposed new university at Vancouver. Not for the last time in provincial affairs, roads and mega-projects were given priority over higher education. (McBride was labelled at the height of the boom as "The Colossus of Roads").

Two events pointed up the gravity of the situation. The most serious was the strike of coal miners on Vancouver Island. When the workers walked out of a number of Canadian Collieries Ltd. operations to protest mine safety and other issues, the response was harsh. The new owners, none other than William Mackenzie and Donald Mann, who had purchased the company from James Dunsmuir, locked the strikers out and brought in scabs to operate the mines. Violence predictably erupted and the government sent in special constables in a vain attempt to restore order. When that failed, Bowser ordered in 1,200 Militia, who promptly arrested 250 strikers. About fifty of these men were eventually jailed, for terms of up to four years. Tension remained high and the Militia stayed in the area for a full year to maintain order, a grim reminder to the public of the state of affairs in the province. The labour support which McBride had previously enjoyed soon evaporated.

The other high-profile calamity was the collapse of the Vancouver-based Dominion Trust Company, costing 5,000 investors their savings. An inquiry revealed that a number of large unauthorized loans had been made by company directors. As in the Principal Trust case in 1987, depositors blamed the government for not excercising regulatory control of the company's affairs. The affair was especially embarrassing for the government because Bowser's law firm was once again in the middle of things, acting for the trust company.

When war broke out in the first week of August, 1914, it gave the beleaguered McBride a welcome chance to forget his troubles on the home front. The lethargy which had begun to show in provincial affairs was cast off and the Premier plunged into the conflict with zest.

• • •

Through his friendship with Churchill, now First Lord of the Admiralty, and devotion to the Empire, McBride had for some time been concerned with naval affairs. Acknowledging McBride's gift of a grizzly-bear rug, Churchill expressed the hope that the Premier would put pressure on Borden in the national debate over whether Canada should build her own navy. McBride sided with those who advocated providing more assistance for the Royal Navy, as favoured by Churchill. The Premier referred disparagingly to Laurier's proposed home fleet as a "toy navy," and was aggrieved by Borden's political waffling on the issue. "I am a Conservative," McBride declared, "but I am a Britisher before I am a Conservative." Little did McBride realize that before long he would be contributing, on his own, two "toys" to the Canadian fleet. In the meantime he jumped in on his own initiative to act as intermediary between the Canadian government and the Admiralty. He did not hesitate to tell Borden what should be done.

When war erupted there was panic on the west coast. Victoria and Vancouver banks instantly moved their cash reserves to Interior branches. Rumours spread that three German cruisers were poised menacingly offshore and there was only the ancient *HMS Rainbow* and a few shore batteries to fend them off.

McBride was in a state of high excitement. On July 29, when war seemed imminent, he was advised of the presence in Victoria of James V. Paterson, president of the Seattle Construction and Drydock Company. During conversation with friends and business associates at the Union Club, Paterson let it be known that he happened to have two submarines for sale which might interest the Canadians. McBride jumped right in, calling a series of meetings to carry out the negotiations.

He was unconcerned that the Chilean government had originally contracted to have both subs built for $818,000 and had later refused to accept them on the grounds that they were unseaworthy because they had not been built to specifications. Paterson was now asking $575,000 for each submarine. When intermediaries for McBride protested, Paterson refused to bargain. Take them or leave them, he said, knowing the vulnerable Canucks were most anxious to obtain the subs.

When officers at the Esquimalt naval dockyard sought approval from headquarters in Ottawa for the purchase, the answer was slow in coming. Too slow for McBride, who decided prompt action was required. The United States government was about to proclaim a Neutrality Act which might complicate the sale of the subs.

McBride's decision to go ahead with the purchase on his own, with unauthorized provincial funds, set off a series of events that have been likened to a comic opera. After a skeptical Paterson was convinced the money would be forthcoming, he agreed to deliver the two subs across the international boundary in Juan de Fuca Strait to a point seven miles southeast of Victoria and eight miles inside Canadian waters. Before they were to sail, however, Sub.-Lieut. T.A. Brown of Esquimalt was sent to Seattle disguised in some old clothes he had borrowed from a navy cook. His assignment was to make sure there were no German agents mingling with the pick-up crew Paterson had assembled for the delivery.

Under cover of darkness, at 10 p.m. on the night of August 4, the two subs left Paterson's shipyard without clearance papers for their rendezvous with the Victoria steam tug *Salvor* in the Strait. Aboard the tug was Lieut. Bertram E. Jones, who was to inspect the subs at sea before formally accepting delivery. Jones was also carrying a cheque for $1,150,000 drawn by the Province of British Columbia on the Bank of Commerce and endorsed by McBride.

After scrambling around the subs for two hours while Paterson looked on impatiently, Jones handed over the money, the White Ensign was hoisted on the masts, while all hands stood at attention and three cheers were given for the King. The subs then headed for Esquimalt harbour, where McBride was waiting to greet them.

Unfortunately, the navy had neglected to inform the army-manned shore batteries of the impending arrival. When the subs were first sighted steaming off the Victoria waterfront, the army went on full alert. Sirens wailed and panic-stricken citizens rushed to the Beacon Hill Park cliffs to watch the battle. Before opening fire, however, some thoughtful shore battery officer telephoned Esquimalt to see if anyone there knew what was going on. An embarrassing calamity was averted.

Two days later the Dominion Government took McBride off the hook by assuming responsibility for the purchase and promptly turning the subs over to the British Admiralty. That was not the end of the affair, however. Despite the perceived state of emergency existing on the coast, questions were inevitably raised about the propriety of McBride's decision to go ahead on his own, the *modus operandi* of the purchase, and the transfer of the subs. There were also doubts about the amount paid and the value of the two craft, which were scrapped in 1920 after the engines burned out in a voyage to Halifax in the last year of the war.

In February of 1915 the Liberals in the House of Commons alleged that McBride had "taken it upon himself to force the hand" of the Borden government. Because financing of the deal was still murky, it was also suggested that McBride had made a profit for the provincial Conservative party. A subsequent Royal Commission found however that McBride had acted properly and the only commission, $40,000, was taken out of the purchase price by Paterson. (Paterson testified that the money was not actually a commission but rather "a kind of a flotsam that came into my possession and remained there.") Despite contrary evidence, the Commission also discounted allegations that the subs had been sloppily constructed.

Although praised by Borden for his actions and completely exonerated by the inquiry, McBride was deeply hurt by what he considered to be attacks on his patriotism. Although he had been in the middle of many political disputes in the past and had shown a remarkable coolness under fire, McBride reacted in this instance with uncharacteristic bitterness. He complained that he was the victim of malicious and venomous attacks by "Grit villifiers" in the Liberal press. Private detectives had been hired by the Liberals to investigate details of the sale and wreck his political career, McBride said. (Which was an ironic twist, since McBride himself was said to have hired Pinkerton agents to keep tabs on his own cabinet ministers.)

The Gilbert and Sullivan aspects of the submarine caper were compounded by other developments at the Dockyard at the same time. Due to the absence of Commander Walter Hose aboard *HMCS Rainbow*, the man in charge was Lieut. Henry B. Pilcher. The pressure of his responsibilities was too much for poor Pilcher when the war began. As well as dealing with a deluge of alarming messages from Headquarters in Ottawa, Pilcher was kept on the hop by McBride over the subs. Paterson remarked in his testimony to the Royal Commission that Pilcher looked "very ill" while the transfer was taking place off Victoria. Pilcher was in fact suffering a nervous breakdown. His behavior indicated that he suspected German agents of running loose on the streets of Victoria. McBride informed Borden that Pilcher was "entirely unfit for duty."

Pilcher was quickly replaced, but for a few days McBride took charge of the Dockyard, a role he obviously relished. Knowing his political fortunes were on the decline, the Premier threw himself whole-heartedly into the war effort. He took an active role in promoting recruitment and bolstering civilian morale, and was responsible for sending 25,000 cans of B.C. salmon to the Front in Europe.

• • •

The war may have been a diversion for McBride, but it offered no escape from his problems; in fact it only made them worse. The railway contractors were having a bad time and they looked to their government benefactors to bail them out. The Canadian Northern was in deep financial trouble and the infamous duo of Mackenzie and Mann spent much of their time camped on McBride's doorstep. At one point McBride sent a telegram to Mann pleading with him to lay a little track "and carry on so as to at least keep up appearances."

After pointedly reminding the Premier that if they were

not able to complete the line to the coast the government would be stuck with heavy interest charges, the pair succeeded in squeezing out another $10,000 per mile subsidy. McBride also managed to persuade Ottawa to increase its aid to the CNR, but the province was still stuck with $48 million in bond guarantees.

McBride's deepest concerns, however, were about the PGE. Contractor Patrick Welch was falling behind schedule while spending far in excess of his budget. The parent firm of Foley, Welch & Stewart refused to put in any of their government-subsidized profits, turning instead to McBride for still more help.

The government could not legally advance money to Welch until work on each section had been completed, but McBride was in a bind. There were already hundreds of unemployed men on the streets of Vancouver, casualties of the recession, and the Premier did not want to see another 7,000 PGE labourers joining the bread-lines. In a calculated political gamble, he decided it was better to keep the job going whatever the cost and authorized payments from the trust fund for work still in progress. Eventually more than $5 million was paid above the value of actual construction. The total bond issue for the 480 miles had all been given to the contractor, however rails were laid only from Squamish to Clinton, a distance of 167 miles. That didn't stop the promoters from celebrating the arrival of the first official train in Lillooet on February 22, 1915, with McBride aboard, smiling as benignly as ever.

Welch was able to push the line a bit further north to Clinton before going broke. That was the end of construction for the next five years, when the government took over the line after paying hundreds of thousands of dollars in interest on the bonds it had guaranteed. In the meantime the affair had helped bring about the demise of the McBride government.

In March of 1915 Foley, Welch and Stewart asked the Premier for another $5 million loan to enable them to continue work on the line. McBride reluctantly agreed but was dismayed to find that a number of his caucus members, led by Bowser, strongly disagreed. They could see that the jig was up, that it was time for the government to retrench. It was the first time in his twelve years in office that McBride had been openly challenged and he was angry. He decided to bring the rebels into line by calling an election, which he did on March 6, setting a date of April 10. "The Government will appeal to the electorate for another endorsement of its bonds on its general record," he declared, "but more particularly for the reason that it proposes in the future attacking vigorously and courageously those features of Provincial development which, though already initiated, are still incomplete." He was referring specifically to the troubled railways and could not see, or would not admit, that the heady days were over. The provincial debt of $10 million was now dwarfed by the government's responsibility for $80 million in railway bond guarantees.

But then McBride lost his nerve. Belatedly he seemed to become aware of the widespread public disenchantment with his government and lack of sympathy for the railway buccaneers. Bowser made it clear that he would not back down and McBride realized he had no alternative but to postpone the day of reckoning. Miraculously, it was discovered that the Lieutenant-Governor had not signed the dissolution papers and so the government was able to cling to office.

But instead of knuckling down to the task of attempting to shore up his tottering administration, McBride amazingly set off on his annual jaunt to England. Scandals were erupting on all sides and Bowser was left to deal with them. It was not an easy task. As in 1907, two high-profile cabinet ministers had been forced to resign in two separate scandals. Price Ellison, the Okanagan cattle baron, quit as Finance Minister after the embarrassing disclosure that he had purchased twelve valuable cows from the government farm at Essondale for $25 each. The farm was under the jurisdiction of Provincial Secretary Dr. Esson Young, who was himself forced to retire in 1915 when it was disclosed that he had been given $105,000 in shares for helping a coal mining company in its dealings with the government.

By this time Bowser was in effect premier of the province. He ruled with a heavy hand, crudely dealing out patronage and stifling opposition in a manner foreign to the ways of the silky smooth McBride.

Three months' socializing in England seemed to revive McBride's spirits and he returned with renewed complacency about the state of the province's affairs. It soon became apparent, however, that he had lost touch and was unaware of the depth of voter unrest and the fast-growing reform movement. Bowser had obviously not kept the Premier informed of developments, perhaps deliberately since it was now assumed the Attorney-General wanted the perks of the top job for himself to compensate for the obligations he had assumed.

Opposition to the the McBride government was fanned by a pamphlet, *The Crisis in British Columbia*, which had been published by the Ministerial Union of the Lower Mainland, a group of progressive churchmen who claimed to be the "moral leaders of the people." The thirty-two-page tract was written anonymously by a disaffected former B.C. civil servant, Moses Cotsworth, who had made a name in Britain as a statistician and economist before emigrating to Canada. Cotsworth called for a federal investigation into charges that land speculators had received information a year in advance on where government and railway surveyors would be working.

Newspapers in the province and across the country picked up on the allegations of the pamphlet and fed the fires of public indignation. The Toronto *Globe* said British Columbia had been "debauched, violated and defiled beyond the limit of endurance." Britton Cooke, editor of *Canadian Colliers Weekly*, compared the machine politics and blatant patronage of the province to that of New York's infamous Tammany Hall. "The real expression of political feeling in British Columbia is throttled before it can be born," Cooke wrote in 1913. "William John Bowser holds his thumb on the political windpipe of the young province."

While McBride was content to dismiss the charges against his government as "mere twaddle," and Cotsworth as a "very adroit but unscrupulous man" with a grudge against the government, Bowser launched a full-scale assault on Cotsworth and his church backers. On July 29, 1915, he addressed a large audience at the Orpheum Theatre in Vancouver, condemning Cotsworth as a revengeful "meddlesome old man who wanted to place himself upon the throne as the Pooh Bah of the civil service." The clerics, "deceived by this designing man," should be serving their country in its time of crisis instead of taking up a partisan political cause. Bowser's blustering antagonism only increased antipathy to the government.

Ordinarily a pamphlet of that nature would have little far-reaching effect on a government, but in this case the timing was critical. Cotsworth's attack came when the government was already staggering and amounted to a knock-down blow from which it could never recover. Its publication provided a focus for widespread public disenchantment.

And so a long summer of unusually glorious weather turned into a bleak political fall for McBride. His appearance on October 4 before the federal commission investigating the purchase of the submarines did little for his morale. At last he could see the writing on the wall and his long-standing equanimity gave way to testiness with his associates and staff. The idea of defeat had not been entertained by McBride for 12 years and as the crunch approached he was too proud to face it. He decided to resign and let Bowser captain the sinking ship alone.

On December 15, his forty-fifth birthday, Richard McBride left his office to take on the much humbler job of B.C. Agent-General in London in the grand new B.C. House, succeeding another ex-premier, John H. Turner. (McBride had been miffed with Turner for turning down the offer of an honorary award which the British had wished to confer on him the previous year and had offered profuse apologies to Westminster). Three weeks later McBride set sail for England with his wife and six daughters.

There are strong indications that McBride intended to return to politics in some capacity and regarded the Agent-General's post as only temporary. It is known that he had been tempted to emulate Joe Martin by seeking election in the Old Country. He had been pressed to do so as early as 1910 by British MP J. Norton Griffiths, who wanted McBride to join a proposed Imperial Party whose members would include Winston Churchill. Griffiths assured McBride that he could "wipe the floor" in debate with Prime Minister Lloyd George and become a new Disraeli. McBride politely declined the offer. Griffiths' flattery was suspect, since he headed a major British construction company which had a number of contracts in Canada and B.C. and was undoubtedly on the hunt for more.

More probable was McBride's interest in the Canadian House of Commons. A letter to him from Prime Minister Borden in November of 1915 indicates McBride had told him of his intention to stand in the next general election. Borden welcomed the news and offered to put McBride in the Senate in the meantime.

But it was not to be. In May of 1917 McBride was ousted as Agent-General by the new Liberal premier, H.C. Brewster, who wanted to reward one of his own party faithful. Brewster was apparently unaware that McBride, who told friends that he would now return to B.C. to resume the practice of law, was in failing health. He had been stricken with Bright's disease and was losing his eyesight. McBride asked for financial help from the Liberals to return home and it was proffered, but he died in London on August 6, 1917, just before he was scheduled to sail. He was forty-seven.

• • •

McBride died a poor man. Never wealthy, he had lost on his small investments when the economy skidded just before the war. His large personal debts at that time inevitably fueled rumours of bribes and payoffs. But McBride simply lacked business sense and was naive about economic affairs, having too much faith in human nature and assuming everyone he dealt with was trustworthy. It was a fatal weakness for the premier of an expanding province which was a feeding ground for boardroom sharks. As Britton Cooke observed, McBride was "helpless as a blind kitten before a mastiff when it comes to facing the demands and blandishments of Sir Donald Mann of the Canadian Northern."

Everything had come too easily for Richard McBride. He had an ingrained sense of timing and a flair for the dramatic, invaluable traits for a politician on the rise. But these gifts also tended to make him lazy. He looked wise but in fact read little and studied less. His speeches were mostly unprepared and often disappointing despite his easy fluency. He enjoyed bantering with hecklers and was seldom ruffled. In essence McBride was a genial showman, charming, affable and guileless.

His main weakness was that he had no fundamental ideas,

only a desire for office, power and adulation. His conservatism was purely pragmatic and was unconcerned with moral issues in public affairs. The public had wanted McBride to introduce party politics to stabilize provincial politics so he called his group of supporters Conservatives. But he had no idea how to construct and operate a political party. That job was left to Bowser, who kept a firm hand on the tiller while McBride kept the voters drowsily content. So B.C. was a Tory province under McBride only on election day. There was no Conservative tradition or principle at work.

The parallels between the careers of McBride and W.A.C. Bennett are striking. Both men squeaked into office with a new party and a bare majority, then went on to increasingly large majorities. They called elections well before the end of their terms whether or not there was any real issue. Both were "boomers" intent on opening up the north to industry, McBride with railways and Bennett with the pipedream Wenner-Gren monorail up the Rocky Mountain Trench. "Legislation by exhaustion" was practised by both premiers to push measures through the Legislature over weak Opposition forces with all-night sittings of the House. McBride was the first premier to use the title "Prime Minister" on his office letterhead, a practice eagerly revived for a time by Bennett.

Historian Martin Robin has characterized McBride as "a self-made man of modest background who believed in and propagated the ideology of frontier conquest through private enterprise." The same could be written of Bennett. Both men were bamboozled by financial promoters and regarded successful businessmen as the highest order of society. Bennett differed from McBride only in his determination to keep a tight personal rein on his subordinates.

William Vander Zalm has the same attitude toward self-made men and employs personal charm in much the same manner as McBride. And like McBride he also relies heavily on political intuition rather than hard groundwork.

McBride succeeded for a time because, in Robin's words, his "patriotism and optimism and reflected the buoyant mood of a province on the make." But in the end he proved to have been merely a good-times Charlie.

William Bowser

John Oliver

S.F. Tolmie

T.D. Pattullo

Chapter 5.

Billy, John, Simon and Duff

The task facing William Bowser in his attempt to hang on to office was daunting. The province was beset by a number of economic woes. Some Conservatives believed he should ask a party convention to chart his political course, but he had no time for such nicety. Now that he was premier in title as well as fact, Bowser saw no reason to change the way he had been operating in the last years of McBride's troubled reign. His party was deeply split on this and other issues, including the widespread suspicion that he had knifed McBride in the back.

But "Billy" Bowser was nothing if not a battler. Born in New Brunswick in the year of Confederation, 1867, he was educated at Dalhousie Law School about the same time as McBride. (Bowser was one of four B.C. premiers from the

Maritime provinces. The others were De Cosmos, Brewster and W.A.C. Bennett). After moving West Bowser failed in his first attempt at election but succeeded in 1903. Active in the Masonic Lodge, he built up a formidable political machine in Vancouver. This work was cemented in 1907 when McBride gave him the post of Attorney-General, which meant control over the police and the lucrative liquor trade.

Squat and square-jawed, he soon became known as "the Napoleon of B.C. politics," or the "Little Kaiser." Blunt, brusque and uncompromising, he was a paternalist who knew what was best for the people. McBride's sugary ways were not for Bowser. He was most at home in the backrooms where his toughness could be unleashed. On the platform he never wooed an audience but rather tried to overwhelm, to carry by storm. His words poured out in torrents. In the House he was a hard-nosed debater.

Bowser had been the perfect hatchet-man for a political smoothie like McBride, who tried to keep everybody happy. A master of detail, Bowser thrived on the manipulations of politics. Like a salesman's greeting, there there was no real warmth in his handshake. He never worried about showing contempt for those he considered his intellectual inferiors, and they were many. His political foes (and these too were many, outside and within his party), regarded Bowser as clever, ambitious, arrogant and ruthless. In these and other ways Bowser came from the same rugged mold as another B.C. Tory of a later era who never quite made it into the premier's chair, Herbert Anscomb.

In order to rebuild McBride's cabinet Bowser was compelled to call three byelections in the spring of 1916. The rejuvenated Liberals won easily in Vancouver and came close in Rossland, but the key battleground was Victoria. There Bowser's choice for Finance Minister, mining tycoon C.C. Flumerfelt, was pitted against Liberal leader H.C. Brewster.

Brewster came armed with a manifesto drawn largely from Moses Cotsworth's notorious pamphlet, *The Crisis in British Columbia*. It had helped bring down McBride and Brewster hoped it would do the same for Bowser. He also had the wholehearted support of the haughty Charles Hibbert Tupper, a chip off the old block if ever there was one. Tupper believed that his patrimony entitled him to respect and a place at the top table in the backwoods province where he had settled down to make his pile. Little wonder then that he was piqued when McBride and Bowser declined to pay him court. Bowser had no time for the Tory old guardsmen like Tupper and E.G. Prior, and McBride went along with his chief lieutenant.

As Bowser put it, Tupper "thought that because he was a prominent Conservative he could get whatever he might demand from Sir Richard, and when he could not achieve his own foolish, personal ends he now shows animosity."

That animosity was bared on the last day of the Victoria byelection campaign when Tupper issued an appeal through the Liberal *Victoria Times*: "I ask Conservatives to drive from power this government which has disgraced the Province and which has been the servile tool of adventurers. I ask Conservatives to defeat every minister of Mr. Bowser who shows his head." For good measure, Tupper concluded bitterly: "What about Sir Richard McBride and the Judas Iscariot who sold him? Who is this Little Kaiser who attempted to read out of the Party Conservatives who dare to have opinions of their own?" So Bowser, once called the St. Peter of Victoria, was now its Judas, although the epithet could easily have been used against Tupper himself for turning on McBride. As B.C. newspaperman and later Conservative party worker Russell Walker has observed, political parties are always defeated by their former supporters.

In any case Brewster was an easy winner over Flumerfelt. Bowser had been given a message by the voters of Victoria. Desperately he attempted to shore up his shaken administration before the general election that must come soon. A number of reform measures were pushed through, including a Prohibition Act which he had previously resisted despite intense pressure from the churches and women's groups. The Act was to take effect July 1, 1917, if approved in a referendum accompanying the election. Another plebiscite was to be held on the question of giving the vote to women, a move which McBride and Bowser had also strongly opposed in the past.

There was a new compensation plan for workers injured on the job, a fund to help returned soldiers acquire land, and loans for farmers. But these and other measures came too late to appease the middle class reform movement which had grown up in opposition to the excesses of the McBride government and as a result of the war, which made people more earnest and righteous. The prohibitionists were not won over by Bowser's change of heart but stayed with their first political allies, the Liberals.

For their part, the Grits under Brewster fought a vigorous campaign, aided once again by the ubiquitous Tupper, who urged the voters to throw the rascals out and restore a true party system to the province, by which he meant his kind of Conservative party. Tupper's stance caused considerable concern among federal Tories. National Party Leader R.B. Bennett urged him not to be "driven into a false position" which would harm the party. Tupper insisted that the election was not a fight between parties "but of people against official wrong-doing," particularly in the field of patronage, from which he had been excluded. Bowser had been "the servile tool of adventurers," he declared.

The Liberals concentrated their attacks on the evils of the McBride administration, repeating over and over the details of various scandals, particularly those involving the railway scams. Liberal J.W. deB. Farris, a bitter enemy of Bowser over the years, accused the Premier of "courting the same old gang of railway promoters that have been robbing the heritage of this province for years." (It was true: the biggest contributor to Bowser's campaign fund was the PGE.)

Bowser got a lift when it was revealed that the self-righteous Liberals were not above a little hanky-panky themselves. A legislative committee uncovered the fact that Malcolm A. Macdonald had ensured his Vancouver byelection win for the Grits by rounding up dozens of down-and-outers on the Skid Roads of Vancouver and Seattle, paying them each $10, and busing them to the polls where they voted in the names of registered electors who had died or left the province. Macdonald's margin had been so great he did not need these illicit votes, but the Liberals had taken no chances. The affair was especially gratifying to Bowser, who had endured many gibes such as that of Liberal stalwart John Oliver about his Vancouver political machine: "When a man obtains money by false pretences he is placed behind prison bars, but when a man obtains the votes of the people by false pretences he is made attorney-general.''

But such minor scandals had little effect on the outcome; the voters had decided they wanted no more of Bowser's brand of Toryism. When the votes were counted after the September 14 election, the Liberals had elected twenty-seven members and the Conservatives just nine. Bowser hung on for another two months waiting for the overseas military vote, but it had no effect on the result. The McBride empire was ended.

• • •

Harlan Carey Brewster was sworn in as premier on November 23, 1916. Prudent and energetic, he had made a small fortune in the salmon canning business. An active Baptist layman, he was regarded as a dull politician, but honest and conscientious. He set out to bring sound, efficient government to a province where those virtues would be a novelty.

Brewster got off to a good start with his cabinet appointments. John Oliver, a veteran of nine years in the Legislature, took over the ministries of Agriculture and Railways. Thomas Dufferin Pattullo became Lands Minister and John Duncan MacLean was Provincial Secretary, while John Hart became Finance Minister. All four men later served as premier.

Brewster happily brought in Bowser's prohibition measure and women's suffrage, both of which the voters had endorsed, and a number of other reform measures, including the introduction of a minimum wage. The most significant of the changes was the creation of a Civil Service Commission that supposedly put an end to the more blatant forms of patronage. But not before the Liberals had ousted scores of Tory office-holders and put in their own supporters. As Railways Minister Oliver explained, ''the Liberals have not had a 'look in' for fourteen years,'' and this was their chance.

Brewster did not have an easy time with the task he had set himself. The province's finances were in a shambles and much of the time of his first months in office were spent in partisan inquiries and sniping over past misdemeanours. And he was soon faced with a scandal involving one of his own cabinet. Attorney-General M. A. Macdonald, who had survived the earlier imbroglio over buying phoney votes in the Vancouver election, was confronted with a serious new charge. The Liberals uncovered the fact that he had received a $25,000 campaign fund contribution from the Canadian Northern Railway Company.

Declaring that he did not want "the slightest suggestion that there is any corporate interest, railway or otherwise, controlling this government," an embarrassed Brewster fired the hapless Macdonald.

In October of 1917 Brewster, frustrated with provincial politics, let it be known that he wanted to enter Robert Borden's Union government as minister of fisheries and mines. He was rebuffed, however, when other members of the federal cabinet pointed out that Brewster had failed to come out in support of the Union government or conscription at the time these were hot issues across the country.

Recognizing Brewster as a weak leader he might be able to rebound against, Bowser was said to have taken a hand in the behind-the-scenes battle to block the Ottawa move. Bowser believed disgruntled B.C. Liberals were pressing to get Brewster into federal politics so they could get rid of him in provincial affairs and find a tough new leader.

The manoeuvring came to a sudden end, however, in March of 1918. Brewster was returning from a conference in Ottawa when he was taken off the train at Calgary suffering from pneumonia. He died there within a few days after little more than a year in office.

• • •

Three members of Brewster's cabinet now sought the vacant Liberal leadership and position of premier: John Oliver, J.W. de B. Farris and Works Minister J.H. King. Oliver won in a close vote.

In a province where premiers have seldom conformed to

the norm of other Canadian jurisdictions, John Oliver was a unique individual. "Honest John," as he became to be known, was a man of the soil, the only farmer to sit in the premier's chair. Heavy tweed suits with baggy-kneed trousers which he was constantly hitching up, solid square-toed boots and cloth cap became the symbols of the man. His speech was simple and often ungrammatical. Rotund and bearded, his walk was a waddle.

Oliver was most comfortable campaigning in the boondocks, at farm fairs and church suppers. He was a man with common sense and without pretence. Blunt but kindly, with twinkling eyes behind steel-rimmed spectacles, he projected a fatherly image. Unlike other premiers who lunched at the Union Club or the Empress, Oliver preferred to dine at the White Lunch cafeteria on Yates Street because "I like to see and pick what I'm going to eat." How could the people not trust such a man?

As is the case with other politicians of the same ilk, however, Oliver could not help being aware that his image was a plus with the electorate, so he played the part of a country bumpkin to the hilt. "I tell you that the blue denim overalls and the cotton jumper are just as honourable as wearing the broadcloth," he told his elegantly dressed colleagues in the Legislature. But Oliver was a much shrewder man than most people realized. He was politically astute, sharp in debate, and a hard worker.

Oliver had learned about toil as the eldest of nine children of a poor farmer and miner in an English village. As a youth he worked in a Derbyshire lead mine, then on the family farm raising chickens and selling eggs at market. A small inheritance enabled the family to break free of English serfdom and move to Canada. Young John first found work as an axeman for the C.P.R., saving enough money to start a farm on 160 pre-empted acres. He became active in community affairs and was elected to the Legislature as a supporter of Joe Martin.

Not everyone was enamoured of the new member from Delta. A Conservative editor complained that he was "given to long-winded and very ungrammatical attacks upon anyone who does not agree with him; one whose brain becomes inflamed with the noise of his mouth.'' Later on, after he became premier, some of his colleagues complained he was too bossy. Oliver liked to do everything himself, the farmer in charge of his flock.

But Oliver soon discovered that at least half a dozen of his members could not be pushed around. He had, in fact, one of the most fractious caucuses in provincial history. The most biting attacks on Oliver's policies often came from his own benches rather than those of Bowser's Opposition ranks. Bowser himself, however, proved to be far more effective on the opposite side of the House than he had been in the premier's chair. By nature he was a better attacker than defender.

Oliver's bumpiest ride was on the PGE, the little railway that couldn't, with no beginning and no end. As minister of railways under Brewster, Oliver had reluctantly accepted the fact that something had to be done about the PGE. It could not simply be abandoned as some suggested. In fact Oliver at times seemed caught up in McBride's fantasies about the railway, despite a newsman's dismissal of the line as ''a plaything of politicians, a gold-mine to contractors, a bugbear to engineers, and a millstone around the neck of the taxpayer.'' Oliver recognized that the PGE offered a mirage of hope to potential settlers in the central interior. He conceded that extension of the PGE might not be justified economically or the engineering sound, but it *was* good politics.

The contractors had ceased almost all work on the railway by this time and Premier Oliver resolved to take it over as a government enterprise. He dreamed of riding the first train into Prince George, but it was not to be. Oliver began by negotiating a deal whereby Foley, Welch & Stewart, who by now had moved the firm's offices to Seattle, would be released from all contract obligations and would turn over the railway's assets, plus $1,000,000 in cash.

After signing this deal in February of 1918, Oliver subsequently borrowed $18 million for further construction. Rather than add it to the provincial debt of $54 million, he financed the railway as a deferred or ''contingent'' liability. It was a neat trick of book-keeping that W.A.C. Bennett adroitly copied years later.

The PGE provided another embarrassment for Oliver when it was disclosed that John Hart, a director of the railway as well as finance minister, had placed a big insurance contract for the line with a firm of which he was a partner.

The other major problem faced by Oliver at the beginning of his term was what to do about prohibition, which had proven to be unenforceable and was now out of favour with the public. The obvious solution was the route taken earlier by Bowser: a referendum. And so on October 20, 1920, a majority voted against prohibition and in favour of government control of liquor sales in place of the saloons and grog shops of earlier days. The new outlets became known as "John Oliver's drug stores" because of the prohibiton practise of getting a doctor's prescription for liquor. (Bowser observed that it was amazing how whisky had suddenly been found to be the best medicine for so many ailments). The stores soon became a big money-maker for the government and have remained so since.

With that problem out of the way, Oliver decided the time was ripe to go to the people in a general election December 1, 1920. The public was skeptical about Oliver and his discordant band of Liberals, but were even less enthusiastic about the alternative, W.J. Bowser and the divided Tories. The vote was split by a host of independent candidates of various stripes, but Oliver managed to squeak back in. He won 24 of the 47 seats and could count on the support of at least four of the victorious independents. The Conservatives took a respectable 15 seats.

Although the Liberals under Brewster had given women the vote and the right to stand for election, Oliver wasn't keen about them taking part in public life. As far as he was concerned, they were meant to stay close to the hearth. He once complained that women could never make up their minds, and when they did something it was always the opposite to what they had said they were going to do. But Oliver could not ignore the feisty Mary Ellen Smith, widow of a Liberal party warhorse, Ralph Smith, and the first of her sex to be elected to a provincial legislature in Canada. When Mary Ellen was re-elected in 1920 by a huge majority in Vancouver, she naturally felt she was entitled to a cabinet post as her husband had been. Oliver tried to fob her off into the Speaker's chair, but Mrs. Smith would have none of it. Honest John reluctantly capitulated, but only to the extent of making her minister without portfolio, which she gave up within a few months from frustration at being left out of the cabinet's inner workings.

Above all else, Oliver worshipped thrift, prudence and industry. He most admired those men from humble origins like himself, who had made it to the top by dint of hard work and dedication. Like W.A.C. Bennett and Bill Vander Zalm after him, Oliver had little sympathy for those who were thrown out of work by the vagaries of a haphazard economic system, or who could not adapt to the demands of industrialization and salesmanship. They were jobless because of "their lack of shift and thrift." He had worked hard and saved his money and others could do the same. Government aid would be provided for widows and orphans but not layabouts.

Oliver had little sympathy for the unemployed: "What percentage of the unemployed men can you induce to leave the bright lights of the cities and toil on the land, as I have done?" he asked. "How many of these men are willing to go out and clean up the land or dig ditches? I have dug ditches for months, and what was good enough for me is good enough for the unemployed."

Such attitudes lead naturally to a disdain for higher education. Cutting funds for the new University of British Columbia in 1922, Oliver said too many college students were "simply putting on finishing touches . . . it is in the nature of a luxury — beautiful but not productive." (Cynics noted, however that he sent his four sons through university and was proud of it). "We are keeping our children in school too long," Oliver complained, "and we are teaching them too many fads."

It was a theme that he would repeat over and over. In a speech to an audience of Vancouver businessmen he declared there were too many non-producers in the cities. "The business of Vancouver could be handled by half the present number of merchants," the Premier said. "The rest should go to work. There are too many lawyers in our cities. A good many men in the legal profession would be better off chopping wood for a living, and they would be more useful. Too many people right here in Vancouver are wearing broadcloth who should be in overalls. Too many women are in fine dresses when they should be in plain gingham."

Despite his declarations in praise of virtue and toil, Oliver was not above trying to help a friend make an easy buck. One of these was an official of the Olalla Mining Company, which claimed to be capitalized for $8,000,000 and sitting on rich mineral holdings. The friend approached the Premier and asked for government aid to encourage capital investment to develop the area around the little Okanagan settlement.

As his secretary and biographer, James Morton, noted, "it was one of those times when the world looked good to John, and he was less cautious than usual." It seems that no premier in B.C., not even plain old Honest John, has been immune from the McBride pie-in-the-sky syndrome. Although Oliver promised to do what he could to help, it soon became obvious the company had bigger hopes than prospects. Only $10,000 had been spent on the property. Oliver was later needled about being "the agent of a company engaged in fleecing servant girls in New York of their hard-earned wages." Oliver blustered that he had acted only as an old friend of the principals and had made no money himself out of the company. But forever after when he was under fire in the House someone would taunt, "O la, la, John!"

One of the issues on which Oliver was particularly vulnerable was the old bugaboo of patronage. After bitterly attacking the McBride-Bowser abuses of the system for twelve years the Liberals, as noted, put many of their own people into government jobs before introducing a civil service reform measure. But party supporters who had waited so long to get their share of government boodle were not happy with jobs being given on the basis of merit only. They kept the pressure on Oliver and he unapologetically went back to the old ways.

Explaining the turnaround, the Premier told a Liberal Party convention in 1922: "We in the innocence of our hearts passed over to a Commissioner patronage rights that should have been exercised by the members of the government and the representatives elected by the people. The results are not satisfactory, therefore we will either have a change in regard to management of the Civil Service or know why."

With his slim majority, rebellious caucus, and the carpings of Billy Bowser, Oliver had a difficult time running the province. His PGE dream soon turned to dust as incompetence and worse in dealings with the contractors resulted in continual political harassment.

The attacks became so frustrating that the Premier occasionally burst into tears. The Vancouver *Sun* reported that in responding to a thrust from Bowser, Oliver "twice burst into tears, once in defence of the chief engineer of the railways department and the other time because, as he said: 'The leader of the opposition seeks to ridicule me when I am trying to do my very best.'"

But Oliver plodded on, or as he put it, "We'll muddle through it the good old British way." One method he employed effectively to muddy the waters, a perennial favourite of B.C. premiers in trouble, was to blame Ottawa for his troubles. He angrily protested the Dominion government's refusal to help bail him out of the PGE mess, and carried on a vigorous campaign for lower freight rates to the West. And there was always the veiled threat: "I have never advocated separation, but if the grossly unjust treatment Western Canada is subjected to in favour of Eastern interests is to be continued indefinitely, then I do not want to call myself a Canadian."

This tactic worked for Oliver in the June 20, 1924, election, but just barely. The Liberals took twenty-four of the forty-eight seats, the Conservatives seventeen, the new Provincial Party three and Labour three. Oliver was still premier of a minority government, but the voters showed their displeasure by defeating him in his Victoria riding. He was quickly reinstated in a Nelson byelection, however.

Oliver was not the only leader personally humiliated in the election. Conservative leader Bowser lost the Vancouver seat he had held for twenty-one years, bitterly blaming dissident members of his own party for his defeat. The other loser was A. D. McRae, the General Bullmoose of British Columbia politics. McRae had made a fortune in dubious Prairie land sales in conjunction with the notorious tandem of Mackenzie and Mann, before moving to B.C. to invest in the timber industry. He didn't like the way Oliver was running things in the province and thought even less of Bowser, so decided to form the Provincial Party to advance his own interests. He gathered together a motley crew of political malcontents, including gadabout Charles H. Tupper, and while electing only three members gained twenty-four per cent of the popular vote and helped return instability to the province. (The party's slogan had been "put Oliver out and don't let Bowser in.")

Restored to office, the plodding Oliver did not have room or ability to manoeuvre the political shoals and went back to muddling through. Although the voters had narrowly rejected sale of beer by the glass in licensed outlets, Oliver decided to go ahead anyway, leaving the final approval in the hands of the municipalities. Opponents of the move fought bitterly and accused Oliver and Attorney-General Alex Manson of being in cahoots with the brewery interests.

The PGE situation was no better and Oliver was ready at last to give up on the railway if he could, but there were no buyers or takers for the pitiful little railroad that went nowhere. Construction was halted and the unused tracks lay rusting.

But enough Liberals remained faithful to the aging Oliver and in March of 1927 endorsed his leadership. Two months later the seventy-one-year-old Premier was operated on for cancer. On August 17, he died after nine years in office, ranking him behind only Bennett and McBride in length of service.

• • •

The premiership passed now into the undistinguished hands of John Duncan MacLean, Minister of Finance and Education. But the Liberals seemed to come unstuck after Oliver's death and MacLean was unable to glue the pieces back together. When the inevitable election came on July 18, 1928, the Conservatives vaulted back into power with a comfortable majority of thirty-five seats to the Liberals' twelve.

The next premier was Simon Fraser Tolmie, son of Hudson Bay Company factotum William Fraser Tolmie and the first premier born in the province. Young Tolmie was a bear of a man, weighing in at around three hundred pounds, but a political pussycat. He was too soft and indecisive for leadership. As usual with such men who reach political heights, he had been a compromise choice after Bowser withdrew and lawyer Leon Ladner failed to gain a majority at a Conservative party convention in 1926.

It would not have been easy for Tolmie in the best of times, and he had the misfortune to take office on the eve of the worst of times: the Great Depression. Tolmie and his inexperienced cabinet ministers were paralyzed by the economic crisis. There were no government policies to help the unemployed, and few encouraging words. Groping for some answers, Tolmie feebly proposed in September of 1932 that a "union" or coalition government be formed in the province similar to that attempted nationally by Borden during the First World War. Liberal leader T.D. Pattullo, who had succeeded MacLean, was offered a cabinet post but wisely declined. Pattullo was, and remained, opposed to any kind of coalition government. He just bided his time while the government drifted.

His chance came on November 2, 1933, after Tolmie had allowed the government to run out its full five-year term, something wise politicians never do. It is regarded as the mark of an administration in deep trouble, and so it turned out.

The Conservatives went into the election deeply divided. Bowser had been lurking around the edges of the beleaguered Tolmie camp and although opposed to coalition, formed a motley Non-Partisan party to join the fight. The old pol wasn't up to the the rigours of battle, however, and died of a heart attack in the last week of the campaign.

It had become clear by then that the battle was not the traditional one between Liberals and Conservatives but rather the Liberals against a new force in the province, the CCF. The ranks of the Socialist-oriented party had been swelled mightily by the Depression, an alarming trend for the financial establishment. In what would become a ritual exercise at election time for the next fifty years, the press railed against the godless socialists who would perpetrate unknown horrors on the people. The Vancouver *Sun* said the CCF would "force teachers to make all our children uniform little Socialists" and would dismiss all teachers who failed to do so. Such scare tactics have varied little in the years since. There would be no investment capital under a Socialist government and the economy would wither. In view of what had been happening to the economy under free enterprise governments in the early 1930s, the jeremiads had an especially hollow ring at that time.

Another tactic familiar to present-day voters had its origin in the 1933 campaign. Since the Liberals seemed to be the only anti-CCF party with a chance of winning the election, they appealed to Tories not to let the Socialists in by splitting the free enterprise vote. "Conservative businessmen who are fearful of the CCF have their remedy in their own hands," said Pattullo. Some of them must have heeded his warning, because when the votes were counted the Liberals had captured thirty-four seats and the CCF only seven, while the Tories were virtually wiped out. Tolmie could not even hold his own seat in Saanich. Although the Liberals had been out of office for only five years, the emergence of the CCF as the Opposition party marked the beginning of a new era in B.C. politics. Although failing to gain many seats, the party had received an impressive thirty-one per cent of the popular vote.

• • •

Thomas Dufferin Pattullo was sworn in as the province's twenty-first premier on November 15, 1933, after seventeen years' apprenticeship in the legislature. Unlike his predecessor, the weak-kneed Tolmie, Pattullo came bouncing in full of ideas to lift British Columbia out of the economic doldrums. He was an admirer of Franklin D. Roosevelt and hoped to employ some of his nostrums, although he realized he was limited in what he could do in a provincial jurisdiction. He had campaigned on the glib slogan of "work and wages," but did come into office armed with an ambitious make-work program, including a grand new bridge across the Fraser River at New Westminster. Most of his plans could not be implemented without the cooperation of Ottawa, however, and that was not easy to come by.

Although many thought the name was Italian, Pattullo was born in Woodstock, Ontario, of Scottish parents. His father owned the Woodstock *Sentinel Review* and was a staunch Liberal, a friend of the parents of Mackenzie King. Young Pattullo worked on the nearby Galt *Reformer* for a time but was lured to the Yukon with dreams of making his fortune. He did not go out hunting for gold, however, but through Prime Minister Laurier got a job as secretary to the Commissioner of the Yukon and then moved to the Gold Commissioner's office. With his white flannel pants and town jacket he cut a dapper figure in the frontier town of Dawson City in 1897. Pattullo was the kind of man who wanted everything to be just right, including his clothes and well-coiffed hair. He admired precision and efficiency.

His dress and ruddy complexion reflected the combative little gamecock he was. A jutting jaw projected over his stocky body, which always appeared to be in a fighting stance. He was a cartoonist's delight.

After three years of government service, Pattullo decided to go into business for himself, not mining but separating the miners from their money by opening a brokerage business. It seemed an unlikely venture for such an unsophisticated place as Dawson City, but Pattullo did so well that he and a partner decided to open a second office in the promising town of Prince Rupert. Pattullo moved there in 1908 and immediately became active in local politics. He was an alderman within two years and mayor three years later. After losing money in the real estate collapse just before the war, Pattullo began to devote more time to provincial politics. In 1916 he was elected to the legislature and served as minister of lands under Brewster. Prince Rupert would be his political base for the next thirty years.

During the Oliver years Pattullo worked diligently enough in cabinet but seemed even more interested in building political support around the province for himself and the Liberals. He was regarded as an outsider and fought against the domination of party politics by Vancouver interests.

In 1929 his reward came when the twelve members of the Liberal caucus chose him as Leader of the Opposition against the Tolmie administration. He relished the role. Tolmie was easy pickings for the flamboyant Pattullo and he made the most of his advantage. He was not a great debater in the House, however, speaking in rapid gusts of words that were at times almost incoherent. He was addicted to long, pompous words and phrases such as "hypothecated" or "oleaginous saponicity." Wisely, however, he dropped this florid style on becoming premier and the purple passages were replaced by simple declarations.

Pattullo may have toned down his language, but the man remained essentially the same: pugnacious, reckless, cocky, abrasive, garrulous, partisan, blunt and stubborn. But like McBride before him and Bennett after, Pattullo was full of self-confidence and an incurable optimist about British Columbia's destiny. The province was God's chosen place and its future unlimited. "We are an empire in ourselves," he declared, "and our hills and valleys are stored with potential wealth which makes us one of the greatest assets of our Dominion." That was his message to Ottawa and he was not averse to coupling it with the threat of separation: "If I did not think that British Columbia is essential to the hegemony of the Dominion, I would tomorrow move to put the question to the test."

Almost as soon as he assumed office Pattullo was on Ottawa's doorstep, demanding "equal terms" in Confederation and large infusions of money to fund his works programs. He pointed out that British Columbia had more than its share of the country's needy because so many had drifted west in search of work and warmer climes.

The Conservative Prime Minister, R.B. Bennett, was naturally cool toward the demands of this brash upstart Liberal premier from the outback of the country, but Pattullo hoped for better things after Mackenzie King was returned to office in 1935. King proved to be frustratingly cautious, however, always seeking compromise. The two Liberal leaders had nothing in common except vanity. When Pattullo urged that the conferring of British titles be resumed for outstanding Canadians, King replied by condemning "the debasing influence of artificial distinctions aimed at establishing forms of 'privilege.' "

Pattullo objected to turning over the income tax field to Ottawa. He would not sit idly by, he said, while the Dominion government "hamstrung and hogtied" the province. Like many others during the Depression, including Liberal backbencher Gerry McGeer, the maverick mayor of Vancouver, Pattullo flirted with some unorthodox financial theories. Dead set against Socialism and some of the wilder schemes of the day, he did want the state to play a greater role in the economy. Pattullo believed simply that governments had a responsibility to eliminate the abuses of economic privilege.

McGeer was miffed when Pattullo did not take him into the government and relations between the two men were always strained. Pattullo probably realized there would not be space in the cabinet room for two such king-sized egos. And Pattullo scoffed at McGeer's flirtation with Social Credit and other bizarre financial ideas. As historian Margaret Ormsby has noted, Pattullo had "a natural aversion to amateurs — other than himself — offering economic panaceas."

Rebuffed by Ottawa, Pattullo in desperation pushed a "Special Powers Act" through the Legislature which alarmed the business community and some of his colleagues. The Act in effect suspended the powers of the Legislature so that emergency economic measures could be enacted directly by the government if it was felt necessary. Pattullo believed the province should have more financial autonomy and this might be one way to put added pressure on Ottawa. Though the Act was never used, Pattullo was never able to escape the "fascist" epithet which his foes pinned on him. In retrospect the controversy was hardly necessary. Pattullo ruled the Legislature with an iron hand without any special powers and had total command of parliamentary tactics and rules. Nevertheless the Act remained an uncomfortable reminder of his occasional bull-headedness.

Meanwhile, a gold-mining boom in the Cariboo spurred Pattullo's dream of opening up the north. He wanted to annex the Yukon and the western half of the Northwest Territory, calling for a highway and railway link between B.C. and Alaska, pushing for oil exploration in the Peace River area, and urging Ottawa to take over the PGE and incorporate it into the new Canadian National system.

The people apparently approved of Pattullo's tactics and

ideas. When an election was called for June 1, 1937, he was returned with thirty-one seats. The Tories won eight and the CCF seven.

• • •

This was the high point of Pattullo's career. His troubles began the following spring when the government cut aid to municipalities, telling them that they should not have to support the able-bodied unemployed, who could go out and find work. At the same time free transportation out of the province was offered to 1,600 men who had been employed on provincial forestry projects during the winter months under a federal program. But instead of meekly going home to the Prairies, these men congregated in Vancouver, where they protested the lack of relief and took part in a number of violent demonstrations.

Pattullo provoked outrage when he had the RCMP hunt and remove transients attempting to enter the province in railway boxcars from the Prairies.

The Premier was in a combative mood when he left in January of 1940 to attend a federal-provincial conference in Ottawa on the report of the Rowell-Sirois Commission. The Commission had proposed a method of redistributing income among the provinces but would require them to surrender control of personal and corporation income taxes, as well as certain other privileges. The talks collapsed when Pattullo joined Premiers William Aberhart of Alberta and Mitch Hepburn of Ontario in refusing to discuss details of the plan. The trio vigorously protested the loss of provincial autonomy.

When he returned home Pattullo found that he had overplayed his hand. The public was not responding to Ottawa-bashing as it had in the past. Didn't he know there was a war on and the country should be pulling together in its time of national emergency? Pattullo was angry at being accused of disloyalty, and his mood was not improved by the discovery that the only political organization supporting his stand was the Social Credit League, with its voodoo economic quackery. Belying his cherubic appearance, Pattullo lashed out at his critics.

Key cabinet colleagues gave him less than full-hearted support in his hour of need. It was noted that Finance Minister

John Hart seemed especially cool toward his boss. Pattullo blamed the rift with Hart on the government's recent decision to control the retail price of gasoline. The oil companies were outraged by this intervention and the Premier came to believe they had made an alliance with Hart to topple him. "From the time that we passed legislation controlling the price of gasoline," he wrote Mackenzie King, "there has been a constant underground agitation against myself personally . . . this plotting has been in progress for many months, the press constantly boosting Hart and depreciating myself."

Despite his earlier experience as a newsman and previous good relations with the Legislative Press Gallery, Pattullo now became extremely sensitive to newspaper criticism. The Liberal Vancouver *Sun* had given him strong support in the past, but that did not stop him from calling its Ottawa correspondent "an unqualified thug." Publisher Robert Cromie chided Pattullo that he should spend more time worrying about British Columbia and less arguing with Ottawa. When Pattullo told a Toronto reporter, "What I say goes in this province," it was a hollow boast.

It soon became apparent that Pattullo had other problems than Hart and the oil interests. He called a general election for October 21, 1941, convinced the voters would give him an easy victory despite the signs of rupture within the government. He campaigned on little but empty platitudes. The result was a rude shock: the Liberals lost ten seats and now had only twenty-one, the CCF jumped to fourteen with thirty-three per cent of the popular vote, the highest of the three parties, and became the official Opposition again. Even the Tories gained, increasing their seats to twelve. Two of Pattullo's top ministers, Attorney-General Gordon Wismer and Education Minister George Weir, had been defeated. Pattullo, who had just squeaked through in his Prince Rupert riding, was now the leader of a shaky minority government.

Festering cabinet unrest broke into the open. It was spiked by the proposal of Conservative Leader R.L. (Pat) Maitland two days after the election that a three-party coalition government be formed in the province. The CCF leader, Harold Winch, immediately rejected the idea, but a number of Pattullo's ministers, led by Hart and Labour Minister George Pearson, were sympathetic. There were a few resignations, including that of the newly-named attorney-general, Norman Whittaker. The besieged Pattullo filled in a number of portfolios himself, including that of attorney-general, although he was not a lawyer. When Hart came out publicly in support of coalition, Pattullo fired him.

On December 2, two days before the scheduled opening of the new legislature, the provincial Liberal Association held an historic meeting. A resolution calling for a coalition with the Conservatives was voted upon the following day. When it passed by a vote of 477 to 312, Pattullo stalked out of the meeting. Hart was subsequently chosen leader of the party and on December 9, two days after the Japanese attack on Pearl Harbour, Pattullo handed in his resignation and recommended to the Lieutenant-Governor that John Hart be asked to form a new administration.

In an emotional speech to the legislature from his new backbench seat, Pattullo said he had served the Liberals in the House for the past twenty-five years and asked, "Do you think that I could lightly see the Liberal Party disappear as such?"

Pattullo stayed in the legislature for the next four years, complaining that he was a victim of a conspiracy and direly predicting the Liberal party would disappear. A new party was likely to move into the political vacuum that had now been created, he warned. Nobody paid any attention. After his defeat by the CCF candidate in Prince Rupert in 1945, Pattullo retired to his waterfront mansion beside the Victoria Golf Club.

Pattullo's downfall can be attributed to a number of factors, not least his over-weening self-confidence. "I am a professional politician in the right sense of the word," he once said. "Politics is the science of government. A professional is an expert. After my years of experience I am satisfied to call myself an expert in the science of government." That statement revealed little more than a misunderstanding of the political process, something that never can be reduced to a science in a democracy. There are too many variants at work, and Pattullo ignored the most important one of all, the mood and the wishes of the people he attempted to govern.

But the Pattullo who will be remembered was the man who in earlier days cried out — in frustration not tears, for he was no weeper — in the face of opposition in the legislature to his ambitious programs: "These howling pessimists! When I lift up mine eyes to the hills and see the glory of British Columbia, I thank God there's no room for them here." The sentiment would be echoed again and again within a few years by a man who was akin to Pattullo in many ways, W.A.C. Bennett.

• • •

Irish-born John Hart, who now took over as premier, had been a shrewd, cautious financier and he brought this mindset to politics. Hart could be a tough leader, keeping a tight rein on his ministers, but had no appeal to the voters.

In naming his new coalition cabinet, Hart did not feel compelled to divide the portfolios evenly between the two parties, since the Liberals held almost twice as many seats as the Tories. He hung on to the finance ministry himself and appointed Conservative leader Pat Maitland as attorney-general. (Maitland naively assumed that he would get a turn at the premiership sometime in the future of the Coalition).

The Coalition governed effectively during the difficult war years and was rewarded with an impressive election victory in 1945, gaining thirty-six seats to only ten for the CCF. Two years later Hart suddenly announced to the Liberal Association that he intended to retire within two months.

The premiership was passed to another businessman, little known Byron Johnson. His nickname of "Boss" came not from his position but his original Icelandic name of "Bjossi" which was changed to Byron. Johnson was born in Victoria of Icelandic parents. Not elected to the legislature until 1945, he had been an influential member of the Vancouver and Victoria group of Liberal businessmen who had agitated for Pattullo's ouster and the formation of the Coalition government.

Johnson's choice as leader came as a surprise to the public. It had been widely assumed that the mantle would fall on Gordon Wismer, a long-time Liberal who had assumed the post of attorney-general on the death of Maitland. There was also Herb Anscomb to consider. Anscomb became leader of the

Conservatives after Maitland died and Hart surrendered the finance portfolio to him to give the Tories a senior cabinet post. The bull-necked, abrasive Anscomb thought the job of premier should be alternated, even though his Tory party was still the junior partner of the coalition. The Liberals never seriously considered allowing Anscomb to become premier, however, and settled on the bland Johnson instead of the rough, tough Wismer in a bid to maintain Coalition unity. The vote was close, however, 475 to 467. There were just enough fearful Liberals to turn the tide against Wismer.

The Tories grudgingly accepted the genial Johnson, and the Coalition thrived under his uninspired leadership. In the postwar economic boom new pulp mills were built, the huge Aluminum Company of Canada project got under way at Kitimat, roads were started and hydro-electric power grids expanded as revenues poured into the Provincial Treasury. Plans were revived to extend the PGE to Prince George. The press was full of praise for the lucky Premier. It was like the McBride days all over again. The people loved their new-found prosperity and were in no mood for change when Johnson called an election for June 15, 1949. The Coalition captured forty seats and the CCF were reduced to eight, victims of the Cold War era and "Commie" charges laid against labour leaders and Socialists.

But the triumph was a hollow one. The overwhelming victory made both parties, but especially the Liberals, wonder if the Coalition was still necessary. Cabinet bickering increased between the two parties, with the ambitious Anscomb pushing his considerable bulk around as minister of finance.

It dawned on some of the Conservatives at last that they were doomed to second place forever under the present Coalition. Some active young Tories like Davie Fulton, Howard Green, Les Bewley, David Tupper and Robert Bonner — exasperated by the dictatorial, self-interested leadership of Anscomb — began looking around for an alternative. They found their saviour in the unlikely person of William Andrew Cecil Bennett.

W.A.C. Bennett

Chapter 6.

Wacky Like a Fox

Apart from his New Brunswick background, William Andrew Cecil Bennett, the twenty-fourth man to serve as premier of British Columbia, shared only a few traits with the others. As a politician, even a B.C. politician, he was *sui generis*. Although Dave Barrett and Bill Vander Zalm futilely attempted to mimic some of Bennett's successful populist techniques, nobody is ever likely to come close. And a good thing too. Despite the acclaim he received for his electoral successes and the prosperity enjoyed during his record-breaking twenty years in office, the boom times of the 1950s and 1960s aren't likely to be repeated.

His critics claim that Bennett simply lucked in, that his arrival in the premier's office coincided with an economic surge that would have happened without his help. Though this is partly true, it misses the point. He was uniquely the man for the times. Those two decades of unparalleled economic growth demanded a salesman in the top job, and Wacky Bennett was a salesman *par excellence*, with all the best and the worst characteristics of that occupation.

Ever smiling, he had a quick, facile mind unburdened by doubts or philosophy. Brash, zestful, audacious, aggressive — he exuded the confident aura of a "doer," a man of action rather than words. There were words, of course, tumbling out in a torrent of scrambled syntax and unfinished sentences. Written down — not easy for reporters without shorthand — Bennett's speeches made little sense. (Little wonder he resisted demands for a provincial Hansard!). He was prone to mouthing simplistic platitudes, trite homilies and just plain gobbledygook. But hardly anybody noticed, or cared. In the jargon of Marshall McLuhan, Bennett was "hot" in the era before the "cool" medium of television would have made him appear the fool.

There was a single-mindedness about Bennett that made him a success in both business and politics. He brought the same skills to both enterprises. Government was simply another business, albeit a big one, and should be run on business principles.

The key to both was advertising. "All advertising is good, wonderful, powerful," he once declared. A good salesman created in the minds of others the desire for "this or that kind of policy, merchandise or service," whether or not it was in their best interests. One good slogan was worth fifty speeches.

A politician of the marketplace, Bennett had no time for courteous debate or reasoned discussion. At his worst he projected "the vulgarity and gracelessness of a haggling peddler," as B.C. political scientist Walter Young bluntly wrote. Bennett was a philistine, a Babbitt, with no interest in anything but politics in the narrowest sense. His Chamber of Commerce mentality did not grapple with the ideas or theories of politics; only the playing of the game was important.

His lack of substance has made Bennett an impossible subject for biographers. A few have tried to pin down the elusive qualities of the man but none has succeeded. What's left is only to describe his astonishing climb to power and the wild ride he took us on once he got there.

Although he left New Brunswick at the age of eighteen, Bennett, like De Cosmos, had already experienced the heady vigour of Maritimes politics. His ancestors and immediate family had suffered economic adversity, but remained fervent Conservatives. The Grits were always the enemy, not the handful of financiers who scourged the Maritimes and kept it an economically blighted area.

Young Cecil attended debates and meetings to hear some of the great orators of an era when politics was regarded as a means of public service rather than a door to personal opportunity. Bennett later entered the arena in the former spirit, although his obsessive climb to the top indicated a drive stronger than a simple desire to serve his fellow men. His later claim that he felt an obligation to his country because he was too young to fight in its first great war and too old for the second also blurs the truth.

Without dipping too deeply into psychology, it seems likely that Bennett was strongly motivated by a desire to exorcise the shame of a ne'er-do-well father and meet the expectations of his strong-willed mother. The father, Andrew, was a drifter who spent little time with his wife and children. He worked at a number of labouring jobs around the province, but never for long. There are hints he was a hard drinker, which could explain Bennett's life-long abstinence, a rarity in politics.

Spurred on by his devoutly Presbyterian mother, Bennett was a model son. At school in the little town of Hampton he did poorly in English but showed an early aptitude for arithmetic. After completing Grade 9, he left school forever to go to work in a local hardware store. The earnest young man read self-improvement books avidly and ran rather than walked around the store.

After a chequered army career his father returned to the family home briefly when the war ended in 1918, then decided to head west to start a new life in the Peace River. He intended to go alone, but for some unexplained reason eighteen-year-old Cecil decided to accompany his father. Predictably, their brief alliance as homesteaders lasted only a short time. The son left for Edmonton to make it on his own.

Cecil's brother and a sister had become school-teachers, and he had toyed with the idea of going into the ministry. Instead he returned to what he knew best: the hardware business. Bennett took a job as an order clerk for the expanding wholesale firm of Marshall-Wells Ltd. and started running again. Soon he was promoted to the position of assistant to the sales manager. He began wearing the navy-blue serge suits that would become his lifetime attire, and threw himself into work and church affairs.

There was great political ferment in Alberta during the 1920's but Cec Bennett merely dabbled in it while he tended to business. He remained a true-blue Tory through the Depression and had nothing but scorn for the radical new movements that were born of it. Bennett was a reactionary believer in the free market economy even as a young man. He regarded as socialistic any government intervention in business matters, such as Roosevelt's New Deal. Even the modest social reform policies advocated by Tory Prime Minister R.B Bennett, such as unemployment insurance, a minimum wage and limitations on hours of work, he found abhorrent.

Bennett scoffed at William Aberhart, the evangelistic demagogue who latched on to the new Social Credit monetary theories propounded by the British civil engineer, C.H. Douglas. He did admire, however, Aberhart's organizational skills and political tactics.

After a brief stint on his own in the hardware business in Alberta, in 1930 Bennett moved to Kelowna with a small stake to make a new start. He bought an established hardware store and followed the smart salesman's course of joining the Chamber of Commerce, the Board of Trade, the Gyros and the Masonic Lodge, all with an eye to helping his business. (Bennett rose to the rank of "Worshipful Master" of his Lodge).

At the same time he was promoting his own store, Bennett took on the larger role of publicizing Kelowna and the Okanagan Valley. What was good for the Valley was good for the hardware business. Despite his deep feelings on the evils of alcohol, he became a partner in the first winery in the area, without ever sampling its product.

Bennett's re-entry into political affairs came about

through his interest and involvement with banks and the financial system. Within the local Conservative party he joined those who favoured establishment of a central Bank of Canada. When the bank came into being in 1934, the ambitious young hardware merchant decided he wanted to be on the first board of directors. Rather than seek the office through the Chamber of Commerce, which was controlling the selection of directors nationally, Bennett campaigned on his own. It was an unrealistic dream, doomed to defeat, which Bennett took hard. The rebuff soured his attitude toward Ottawa and firmed up a resolve to become involved in provincial politics.

His timing was poor, however, because the Tory government under Tolmie was about to be bounced from office by Pattullo's Liberals. So Bennett bided his time for four years, then decided to seek the Tory nomination for South Okanagan in a provincial general election. An established figure in Kelowna, he was confident of winning in his home territory. It was a crushing blow when Vancouver lawyer Tom Norris beat him out for the nomination. Years later Bennett insisted he had been a reluctant candidate who entered the race only at the urging of the local party executive. But Bennett's memory was simply twisting the truth to enhance his image, a common practice.

This first political rebuff also revealed another side of Bennett: although he worked within the party system, he was not a loyal party man. When Norris asked for his support in the election Bennett turned his back on him and went to work instead expanding his hardware business. He was not disappointed when Norris was beaten by a Liberal.

In the 1941 provincial election Bennett tried again for the nomination and this time was successful. It was the watershed election which brought on the ill-fated Coalition. Bennett was one of twelve Tory members in the new House.

● ● ●

In the flush of his maiden speech in the Legislature, Bennett declared that the Coalition government was opening "a new era of public enlightenment in the government of B.C." He

117

gave the administration his full support because it was headed by John Hart, a man who had made his mark in the financial world and was therefore worthy of respect. Bennett became so carried away by the idea of coalition, in fact, that he urged a permanent fusion of the Liberals and Conservatives into a Coalition Party which would replace the existing uneasy alliance. His colleagues in the House paid little attention to the new member from South Okanagan, who was ignoring the perennial problem of the division between the federal and provincial arms of the major political parties. (Later, in fact — in 1951 and 1952 — the federal organizations of both the Tories and the Grits in B.C. applied pressure to end the Coalition.)

Bennett later claimed that Tory Leader Pat Maitland had offered him one of the party's three cabinet portfolios but he had turned him down. Bennett said he told Maitland that his business and his family required too much time to allow him to accept. In view of the fact that Bennett's vaulting ambition was already obvious, his version of events is highly suspect. A man determined to reach the top could not afford to reject such an unexpected plum so soon after being elected. It is also a fact that there were other Tories with larger claims on the office who Maitland would have to consider before Bennett.

After being returned to the legislature in the 1945 election, Bennett resumed his campaign for a coalition fusion party. His speeches on the subject were redolent of the "non-partisan" rhetoric of Gen. A. D. McRae and his misbegotten Provincial Party of two decades before. Bennett did succeed, however, in establishing such an organization in his own riding, keeping his name in the news in the process. Then Pat Maitland died and it was a new ball game. After Herb Anscomb had manoeuvred himself into the finance portfolio with an eye to taking over as Tory Leader, Bennett promptly dropped his permanent coalition idea and went after the leadership himself. Despite giving away cartons of Okanagan apples to convention delegates, the bumptious Bennett was soundly trounced by Anscomb.

His ambition frustrated now on two fronts, Bennett launched a bitter, scattergun attack in the legislature on the

Coalition government. He condemned Anscomb's new budget as tight-fisted and urged the government to spend, spend, spend. The fury of his criticism was blunted by its lack of a consistent point of view. The House and the press came to regard the maverick member from South Okanagan as a mere nuisance, a political gadfly. His only legislative ally was Tilly Rolston, the Tory member for Point Grey, a widowed Baptist and early feminist. It is difficult to explain Mrs. Rolston's alliance with Bennett, except that she too regarded herself as a rebel and was disregarded by the clubroom cigar-smokers of the Coalition leadership.

Bennett stepped up his attack during the 1948 session following the resignation of John Hart and the anointing of Byron Johnson as premier. When Anscomb brought in a three-per-cent sales tax to help finance mushrooming social service costs, Bennett warned darkly that it would kill business in the province. At the end of the session he abruptly resigned to run for Parliament in a federal by-election in Yale riding, which took in his own bailiwick.

His head in the political clouds, Bennett apparently believed he was about to launch a triumphant career in Ottawa that would carry him to the Tory leadership and eventually Prime Minister. His dreams received a rude shock when he lost the election to the CCF candidate Owen Jones, even though the Conservatives had held the riding for the past twenty-four years.

In the provincial byelection that followed for Bennett's vacated seat, the embittered hardware merchant once again showed the self-serving nature of his political convictions. When the South Okanagan Coalition Association, which Bennett had created, nominated a candidate to succeed him in the legislature, Bennett refused to lift a finger to support him. Bob Browne-Clayton, who won the seat anyway, said Bennett "would not touch me in my campaign, no assistance whatever. He just backed right off, went into a huff, with no help."

When a federal general election was called early in 1949 Bennett sought the Tory nomination again, but was rejected by the convention in favour of Mayor Theo Adams of Vernon. Bennett's later explanation for the rebuff was that he believed

God always answered prayers, "but sometimes His answer is 'no'
. . . I was told very definitely, I think, that my field was not to be
federal politics — I was to go back in the provincial field again."

• • •

It is difficult to imagine God concerning Himself with an
obscure politician in a backwoods election in Yale riding, but
Bennett actually believed he had a special relationship with the
Deity. After an unexpected triumphant election victory in 1969
Bennett was in an expansive mood when he was interviewed at
home in Kelowna by a reporter from the *Toronto Star*. He began
by pointing to a television set and stating the obvious: it wouldn't
work if it wasn't plugged in. "That's why I'm successful in
politics," he continued. "I'm plugged in with God. If I pulled the
plug out I'd be no good either."

Bennett babbled on about the recent spacecraft landing on
the moon being made possible by "waves" in the universe that
had been present for billions of years. "All man has to do," he
said, "is to work to find out what these laws are, of the universe,
and the laws for his life, and instead of balking them, going
getting drunk, and smoking those terrible cigarets, and going out
all night and that kind of stuff, and work with these laws he has
happiness. These are nature's laws, for the universe and for man.
These are God-made laws and they work. They're there all the
time. I know what the natural law is. That's how I'm successful in
the political campaigns. I know what the natural law is and I
work with them."

The veteran *Star* reporter, Jack Cahill, had difficulty
believing the unusual turn his interview had taken with the hyper,
bubbling Premier. It was as if someone had slipped something
into his Ovaltine. Cahill got it all down on a tape-recorder and
was able to refute Bennett's later second-thought denials of
claiming he was plugged in to God.

During their conversation Bennett said the NDP had lost the
1969 election because they had not followed the natural laws of the
universe. The party's new leader, Tom Berger, had gone down to
defeat because he had plotted to replace Bob Strachan in a

leadership struggle. This, Bennett declared, was against the natural law and so Berger was punished for his folly. (There was apparently no such breaking of the natural law, however, when Bennett had tried to unhorse Anscomb years before. That was different.)

Whatever the nature of his special tie-in with God, it did not provide Bennett with the gift of prophecy. He told Cahill that Berger had damaged the NDP so badly that "it will never recover in my lifetime." Three years later Bennett was rudely removed from office by the NDP.

• • •

Acting on God's instructions after his 1949 federal rebuff, Bennett returned to provincial politics as the Coalition candidate for South Okanagan in a general election just six months later. To some his hopping about was sheer opportunism, but Bennett recognized that politics is a game of opportunities. Or rather, a war of opportunities, for he always regarded politics as a field of combat. He eventually became a General because of his unique ability to return to action after wounds which would have been mortal for lesser men. In this he resembled those roly-poly, round-bottomed children's toy figures that lurch back to an upright position after being bowled over.

And so, undaunted by his previous knockdown, Bennett, backed by the young Tory ginger group of Bonner, Bewley, et al, decided to challenge Anscomb once again for the Tory leadership. Although he always boasted of never dealing in personalities, Bennett and his supporters pulled out all the stops in their attack on the imperious Anscomb, who was sometimes referred to behind his back as "Il Duce." It was all in vain. Anscomb's grip on the Tory machine was unbreakable and he turned back Bennett's second challenge by a wider margin than the first.

It was now apparent to all that Bennett had no future with either the crumbling Coalition or the Tories. He was simply awaiting an opportunity to jump ship. It came soon during debate in the legislature over a controversial new hospital insurance plan. After a bitter, ranting indictment of the Coalition government, Bennett declared he was leaving it and stalked out of the chamber.

He would have crossed the floor in the time-honoured gesture, except for the fact there was no seat on the other side ready to receive him. Later he was given one in the back row next to CCF member Leo Nimsick of Cranbrook. It was a significant placement since Bennett, now sitting as an Independent, represented the nether reaches of the province opposed to the power-brokers of Vancouver and Victoria. Nimsick, a pliant, amiable man, gratefully lobbed verbal grenades at the Coalition benches handed to him by his new seatmate.

One of Bennett's first steps after striking out on his own was to persuade a reluctant Tilly Rolston to follow him. Mrs. Rolston was fighting a losing battle with cancer at the time and Bennett's critics have accused him of using her to serve his own political ends. Even her family intervened, asking Bennett in vain to let her return to the Tories.

Bennett's next move left no doubt of his willingness to use people as pawns in his political manoeuvres. In the fall of 1951 a byelection was called in Esquimalt riding following the death of the sitting Coalition member. Bennett scouted the field for prospective candidates to run as an Independent and settled upon Alfred Wurtele, a recently retired navy officer and local alderman. "He was an ideal person," Bennett later recalled, "but he knew nothing about politics." Not to worry. Bennett would tell him all he needed to know. Though Wurtele had no real desire or interest in provincial affairs, he could not withstand Bennett's pressing calls to duty. Later when he changed his mind and tried to withdraw, Bennett did not answer Wurtele's telephone calls to Kelowna or acknowledge his telegrams.

When he finally made contact, Wurtele was told by Bennett that as "an officer and a gentleman" he could not back out of their deal. Wurtele protested that he had no money to run a campaign. No problem. Bennett would finance it out of his own deep pockets.

Once the nomination papers were signed, Wurtele was pushed aside as Bennett took control. He wrote the candidate's speeches attacking the Coalition and delivered some of them himself. The advertising bills which he paid totalled close to $10,000. Wurtele admitted later that he hardly knew what was going on. When the ballots were counted on the night of October

1, the surprise winner was Frank Mitchell of the CCF. Wurtele was a close second and the strong Coalition candidate, Mayor Percy George of Victoria, came in a distant third.

Bennett had made his point, that the Coalition was out of favour with the voters and vulnerable, and was actually relieved that his man had not won. For the decent, unimaginative Wurtele would have been out of his depth in the jungle warfare of the B.C. legislature. He had been cynically manipulated only to facilitate Bennett's insatiable drive to the top.

For the moment Bennett was content to watch B.C.'s political universe unfold and bide his time, waiting for a wagon to come along to jump aboard and grab the reins. The vehicle he eventually chose was a strange one: Social Credit, the "funny money" movement born of C.H. Douglas and nurtured in a peculiar evangelical offshoot in Alberta by the Reverends William Aberhart and Ernest Manning. Bennett conveniently forgot his earlier contempt for Aberhart's version of Social Credit.

Bennett would spend the rest of his political career dissociating himself from Douglas' monetary theories and the undisguised anti-semitism of his most fanatical adherents, but at the time Social Credit seemed the best means of getting him to his destination. By repudiating the Coalition he had set himself up as the leader of a great crusade to purify politics, a cause that tied in with Social Credit's anti-establishment roots. (The Socreds of that period have been described by Martin Robin as "political outsiders whose suppressed envy and frustration was sublimated into moral fervour.")

Bennett's decision to hitch up with the Social Credit "movement" — it did not regard itself as a political party —was greeted with wonderment, even in a province where almost anything goes. When asked by a reporter how he could suddenly become a Social Crediter, Bennett replied in all seriousness, "I studied Social Credit as I studied every political philosophy. I decided I should accept it." Coming from a man who was always too busy with the mechanics of politics to read anything of history or theory, the remark was outrageous malarkey. But it was typical of the self-serving equivocation that Bennett tossed off throughout his career.

The Victoria *Colonist* took a cynical view of Bennett's sudden conversion. It was, the newspaper said, "one of those phenomena of instant enlightenment, a blinding apocalyptic flash of revelation unknown to meteoric science, but fairly common in politics. After advocating Conservative principles all his life, Mr. Bennett wakes up one morning to realize that he has always believed in the very opposite. The veil is torn from his eyes."

The truth was that Bennett had few options. He couldn't achieve his ambitions as an Independent and his chances of forming a new political party from scratch were slim. The B.C. Social Credit League offered a small but well-established organization with a potential for growth. And most important from Bennett's point of view, it was virtually leaderless. He was a political gambler by instinct who looked for favourable odds before taking a plunge. In this instance he knew that as the only Social Crediter with Legislative experience he would be in the catbird seat after the forthcoming election.

Bennett could hardly have expected, however, that Social Credit in its first serious election campaign could achieve a majority of seats. But he knew there were many voters out there disenchanted with the Liberals and Tories and unwilling to vote for the harsh rhetoric of CCF Leader Harold Winch. He was also aware that the transferable ballot, brought in for this election in one of its last acts by the Coalition with the object of keeping the CCF out, would work to Social Credit's advantage. Under this system voters listed their first, second and third choices which were added to the totals in separate ballot-counts as the last-place candidate was dropped until one had an absolute majority. Winch denounced the measure as "one of the most shameful bills ever introduced into any parliament in Canada."

The Coalition finally came apart in January of 1952 when Premier Johnson fired Anscomb as finance minister after a number of provocations. An election was called for June 12, with the two old-line parties fielding separate lists of candidates.

Under Bennett's guidance the Socreds drew up a campaign "program" — carefully avoiding the term "platform," which smacked of politics rather than the people's crusade which they aspired to be. Apart from calling for less government interference with business, the policy paper was composed mostly of generalities and platitudes. One journalist said it "read like the Ten Commandments."

Religion, in fact, played a big role in the Social Credit campaign. Long-time Socred Eric Martin, later to become minister of health, told a meeting of Vancouver businessmen that his group would go to Victoria "with the Bible in one hand and our platform in the other." The candidates included four clergymen (three were elected) and no lawyers. Tilly Rolston told her nominating meeting she didn't know anything about Social Credit monetary theories but simply wanted "a return to honest Christian principles in government."

The crusading flavour of the Socred campaign was imparted in no small way by its nominal leader, the Rev. Ernest G. Hansell of Alberta, a fundamentalist preacher. He had been put in charge, with the acquiescence of the neophyte B.C. party, by Premier Manning's government, which regarded itself as the fountainhead of Social Credit in Canada. Manning wanted to ensure control over the B.C. offshoot. Bennett wasn't pleased by this development, but knew that he would have the upper hand after the election as the only Socred other than Tilly with legislative experience. (Hansell was an MP but could not seek a seat in B.C. because he was not a resident of the province.)

It was a strange campaign. Johnson was no politician at the best of times and had never regained his full energy after being injured in an automobile accident in late 1950. He waged an ineffectual campaign as a caretaker premier, dwelling lamely on the economic successes of the Liberal-led Coalition. Anscomb was more aggressive on behalf of the Tories, but found little support in the rural areas of the province where Social Credit was catching fire.

The voters did not know or care what Social Credit stood for, but most were aware that a government of the same name was apparently performing well in Alberta. They also took to the folksiness of the Socred candidates, homespun amateurs who shunned the pin-stripe suits of the despised Coalition politicos. Dark warnings that the anti-semite aspects of Social Credit raised "the ugly head of Naziism and Fascism" in B.C. were ignored.

If it was an unusual campaign, the election itself and subsequent ballot-counting were positively weird. There were a record 212 candidates in the 48 ridings and results of the first ballot were not known until the following day. They showed that the CCF had captured 34.3 per cent of the votes, Social Credit 30.2, Liberals 25.3 and Conservatives a mere 9.7. If the normal voting system had been in effect, the CCF would have formed a minority government with twenty-one seats and Social Credit become the Opposition with fourteen. But then the interminable recounting of ballots to determine second and third choices began, with the final result in the "hang-fire election" not known for more than a month.

The final result was a surprise to almost everyone. Social Credit had ended up with a slim one-seat edge over the CCF, nineteen to eighteen. The transferable ballot had affected the outcome in an unforeseen way. It had succeeded in blocking out the CCF but did not keep the Coalition in as plotted.

● ● ●

On July 15 the newly-elected Social Credit MLAs met in the Hotel Vancouver, hardly able to believe their good fortune. Bennett was exuberant, bubbling and beaming at high voltage in anticipation of the leadership vote which would vault him into the premier's chair. He won hands down, with fourteen of the eighteen votes. "I knew what was going on in his mind," said Eric Martin. "He had lived for this. Ever since he was a small boy he was going to be the big shot in some political puddle." For himself, Bennett had little to say after the vote, except to caution reporters to "go easy on the (Social Credit) monetary stuff. Remember, it doesn't concern us now."

Lieutenant-Governor Clarence Wallace hesitated briefly, but after pressure from Bennett asked him on August 1 to form the new government. CCF Leader Harold Winch, claiming he had enough support in the House to govern, protested bitterly but in vain.

Bennett set about selecting a cabinet. There were no lawyers in the caucus so he had to look outside for an attorney-general. (Gordon Wismer, ever the wheeler-dealer, volunteered to stay on in the post. It must have given Bennett great pleasure to decline the offer from his old Coalition foe.) He settled on Robert Bonner, his icily urbane young Tory supporter. For finance minister Bennett chose Einar Gunderson, an establishment figure who was meant to reassure the business community. Two undistinguished rural backbenchers were persuaded to resign and open up seats for his appointees. It was a risky move. If either had been defeated in the byelections the Socreds would have lost their one-seat majority over the CCF.

There was no question who was the boss. As Bennett said later of his jerry-built cabinet, "they were a great team because they were all new and so they took advice well." Bennett went to work like a man obsessed, creating the lasting image of a premier single-handedly rebuilding the province's economy. It had been left in tatters, he told the public over and over, by the do-nothing Coalition government.

The truth is that Bennett came into office on a postwar tide of economic expansion and government revenues that was already in flood. The private sector was growing giddily, led by the huge Aluminum Company of Canada projects at Kitimat and Kemano which had been negotiated by the Coalition. There was a new oil pipeline from Alberta to Vancouver and forestry was flourishing as U.S. investment soared. During the decade of Coalition rule the population of the province had risen by more than twice the national average and wages were the highest in the country.

Fueled by unprecedented revenues, the former government had embarked on a huge spending spree, building roads and bridges all over the province. Bennett merely carried on and later accelerated this work. He also continued, but claimed for his own, Premier Johnson's "pay-as-you-go" policy of financing public works out of current revenue instead of borrowing as in the past. Later Bennett would abandon the policy with sleight-of-hand bookkeeping designed to disguise borrowing.

In February of 1952, four months before the election, *Macleans* columnist Blair Fraser, who later that spring helped bring down the Coalition by exposing the corruption of the Liberal party machine in Vancouver, reported that "the province has never been so prosperous — it even out-booms Alberta.'' But in a 1975 interview with the same magazine, Bennett declared that when he came into office British Columbia was "the number-one 'have-not' province in Canada.'' He had come to believe his own propaganda.

On November 1, 1952, Bennett rode the first PGE train into Prince George just as if the railway extension was his own idea. Former premiers Hart and Johnson were not invited to the ceremony. It was an early example of the pettiness and lack of courtesy that would mark the Bennett regime. Members of the Opposition or federal government officials were never invited to such affairs during his twenty-year term of office.

Although the controversial B.C. Health Insurance Service was in good working order when he took over, Bennett refinanced the scheme to eliminate premiums by raising the provincial sales tax from 3 to 5 per cent, despite his furious opposition to the original tax.

Most of Bennett's backbenchers remained silent during the legislative session in obedience to their boss. Only J.A. Reid of Salmon Arm created a stir by sounding off about immoral, socialistic textbooks in the schools. Finally, on March 24, 1953, Bennett succeeded in engineering the defeat of his government on the floor of the House with a relatively obscure vote on education funding. In the ensuing election, which Bennett proclaimed in typical hyperbole as "the most important ever to be held in British Columbia,'' the Socreds were returned with twenty-eight seats to fourteen for the CCF and four Liberals.

The only setback for Bennett was the defeat of Einar Gunderson, who after losing in another byelection a few months later went back to the boardroom and served Social Credit in the future only as a fund-raiser. Bennett took over as finance minister. The election also made clear that the transferable ballot, which had brought him into power, had lost its value to Bennett. Second choices actually took two seats away from the Socreds. At the next session in November, on the dubious grounds that it would be "unfair" for the CCF to gain power with only 35 per cent of the vote, he abolished it. Bennett had no problem with the possibility that Social Credit might be elected in the future by a minority of the voters.

• • •

As he set about implementing his economic agenda, Bennett found the legislative process a nuisance. His answer was to keep the sessions as infrequent and short as possible, resulting in a diminished role for the Opposition, which had no money or offices between sessions.

Controversial legislation was introduced in the waning days of a session and sittings were extended beyond the normal adjournment time — "legislation by exhaustion." The result was a dismaying increase in personal frustration and invective. While Bennett rested in his office, weary members, including some of his own cabinet ministers, would return to the bearpit well-fortified by prandial drinks. Debate was reduced to a snarling match of insults which the Speakers selected by Bennett were unable or unwilling to curb. It was the beginning of the politics of polarization and confrontation which have continued to the present day.

Under fire, Bennett's standard response was to jeer. "All the opposition can do is smear, smear, smear," he shouted. "All it can talk is fluff, fluff, fluff." Questioners were carping critics who threw sand in the gears. Those phrases were repeated over and over, especially during the four or five times that Bennett rose during a session to launch a wild, arm-flailing, sputtering attack on the Opposition. It was good circus, if nothing else.

Bennett's tirades against Opposition leaders and critics were often harsh. He talked piously of the importance in a democracy of political opposition, but his earlier opportunistic behaviour in that role belied his words. Bennett's contempt for parliamentary rules and the tradition of courtesy and cooperation distinguished him from a true conservative. That breed was virtually extinct in the House. Bennett's most effective foe was Liberal Leader Arthur Laing. An able parliamentarian and debater, Laing was able to get under his skin. Bennett, he said, appealed to prejudice with "flippancy, petulance, ridiculous bombast." In a moment of anger at being subjected to Bennett's demeaning tactics, Laing glared across the floor and told the beaming Premier: "You are a phoney!"

Laing eventually gave up in the face of Bennett's relentlessly bizarre style of politics and turned to the federal field, where he became a respected cabinet minister. Bennett's secretary, Ron Worley, who later wrote a fawning book about his boss, said that of all the Opposition leaders Bennett faced over the years the one who impressed the Premier least was Laing, dismissed as "not a worthy opponent." Like almost everything else in Worley's hagiography, the comment rings hollow.

Worley was one of Bennett's few social intimates during his twenty-year residence in Victoria as premier. He was truly "the loner from Kelowner," as dubbed by MLA Tom Uphill. In the beginning when Bennett was resented by some old-time Social Crediters for taking over their organization for his own use, Worley referred to them as old dodderers. "The inexperience and stupidity of some of these characters is most appalling," Worley told Bennett. Lyle Wicks, a future cabinet minister, he described as a "wretched little man."

Another Bennett friend was Waldo Skillings, a former amateur boxer with a hair-trigger temper. Skillings once referred to the old-time Socreds as "goons." He frequently scuffled with hecklers at Bennett meetings and on one occasion got into a shoving match with a CCF member of the Legislature in the Speaker's Corridor. As newspaper publisher Stuart Keate observed: Bennett's friends "seemed as far removed from him in personality and character as one could imagine."

As he did with the Opposition, Bennett paid lip service to the role of the press but treated his relations with it as a game. Although the newspapers invariably ended up at election time supporting Social Credit against socialism, Bennett regarded them as hostile. Keate revealed in his memoirs that Bennett once complained to Victoria *Times* owner Max Bell that Keate and editor Bruce Hutchison should be fired because they were "menaces to good government." The Premier also approached newspaper magnate Roy Thomson in London and asked for the support of Thomson's small-town newspapers in B.C. because the metropolitan press was so negative.

Bennett's other running battle was with Ottawa, a tradition with B.C. premiers. Bennett liked to pretend that he took the high road in relations with the federal government. When Duff Pattullo was fighting with Ottawa, Bennett criticized him for walking out of a federal-provincial conference. Pattullo was a great British Columbian, he said, but "you must be a Canadian before you are a provincial premier."

Once again, Bennett's actions belied his words. He didn't stalk out of any conferences, but the British Columbia chair was often conspicuously empty at national meetings. When he did deign to attend or send a cabinet minister in his stead, B.C. always had the smallest delegation. For Bennett, Confederation was simply a matter of economics. A materialist, the only aspect of federal-provincial relations that interested him was finance. Constitutional issues were boring. He assumed Quebec had no other reason for pressuring Ottawa than he did — to get more money. Bennett was out of touch with social issues and concerns that arose in the 1960s. Refusing to recognize any national problems, Bennett tried to talk about federal subsidies for B.C. highways. He became a national joke and an embarrassment to many British Columbians, merely amusing to others.

At one conference Bennett said Ottawa should get out of the income tax field, one of the cornerstones of Confederation. His idea was bluntly rejected. While agitating for a provincial bank Bennett told a Senate committee that the only reason he went into politics was because he saw too many businessmen being refused loans. When the Senate also rebuffed him, Bennett peevishly threatened secession.

The Premier made one serious foray into federal politics when in the early 1960s he perceived an opportunity to make hay from the delicate minority government balance in Ottawa. Allying himself with the flamboyant Quebec car dealer and Creditiste leader Real Caouette, Bennett attempted to seize control of the national Social Credit party from Ernest Manning. The Alberta premier was supporting local boy Robert Thompson for national leader. Caouette's forces won twenty-six seats in

Quebec but his wild views frightened the majority of Social Crediters across the country and Thompson was chosen. Never a gracious loser, Bennett bowed out after that setback and was petty in his dealings with Thompson thereafter.

Bennett's belligerence toward Ottawa and political enemies at home came together in the controversy over the Columbia and Peace River development projects. Although Davie Fulton had once been an ally in the B.C. Conservative party, the federal spokesman was now regarded by Bennett with hostility. One close observer of the affair has suggested that Bennett's vendetta with Fulton went so far as to influence his policy moves on the Columbia. Later, when Fulton made a misguided return to B.C. politics in an attempt to unseat Bennett, he suffered a humiliating defeat. He was yet another intelligent, civilized politician who could not cope with Bennett's steamroller tactics.

The Columbia negotiations were a complicated, three-way affair between Ottawa, Washington and Victoria. At times Bennett seemed to take a stronger position against the government of his own country than he did with the U.S., especially when he injected the "two-river policy" involving the Peace into the the dispute. Gen. Andrew McNaughton, the Canadian chairman of the International Joint Commission, said that decision by Bennett helped the Americans, who "walked in on a house divided against itself and skinned the occupants alive."

Academic economists plowing through a maze of figures are still arguing whether the Columbia Treaty was a good deal for Canada. Some say Bennett was more interested in the financing than the engineering of the project. One of the interesting political sidelights of the affair was the harsh criticism of Liberal Pat McGeer. Bennett's hydro strategy was based on politics rather than economics, McGeer said, and "the greatest myth that has ever been perpetrated on the people of British Columbia is that there is cheap power in the province." The Americans were the "big winners" in that their industries got cheaper power and B.C. a lot of flooded farmland for its troubles.

McGeer's criticism of Bennett and Social Credit didn't end with the Columbia. Noting that B.C. spent less per capita on post-secondary education than any province in Canada, McGeer said Bennett complained every year in his budget speech about the rising costs of education, while boasting of huge expenditures on hydro-electric developments. Funds were made available for these projects at the expense of municipalities and school and hospital boards. In pursuing these projects, McGeer noted, the government showed no interest in environmental protection. Ravaging the landscape, he said, was "deeply rooted in Social Credit's idea of progress."

More serious was McGeer's charge that Bennett had also ravaged the political process. "Over these last twenty years in this province," he wrote in a 1972 book, "we have elected, and re-elected again and again, a premier and an administration who have adopted an attitude of scorn for the accepted political decencies, and of contempt for the proper processes of government and of law whenever these things have stood in their way . . . public morality in any true sense cannot be said to exist in British Columbia today."

Three years after this devastating critique, McGeer, with three of his Liberal colleagues, joined the Social Credit party to become cabinet ministers in the government of Bennett's son.

• • •

W. A. C. Bennett's twenty years in office were dogged by one scandal after another, but by election time the public had either forgotten or didn't care. Bennett was a master at muddying the water with diversionary tactics which confused the opposition parties, reducing them to an impotence that the voters perceived and rejected. When the going got tough, there was always the bogeyman of socialism to be dragged out.

The most notorious scandal was the protracted Sommers affair. Robert Sommers was a Kootenay school teacher who had a taste for high-stakes poker. Named by Bennett as minister of lands and forests in the first Socred cabinet, Sommers was soon in trouble. Accusations were made that he had accepted bribes in connection with the granting of valuable forest management licences to large timber companies.

Sommers promptly filed libel and slander suits against his

accusers. With skilled bafflegab legalese and evasion, Attorney-General Bonner convinced the public that no legislative or police action could be taken until the civil suits were settled. The whole affair was *sub judice*, out of bounds to debate, Bonner said. For two years the government sat on the case in this devious manner. In the meantime Bennett called an early election for September 19, 1956, with the slogan, "Progress not Politics." He won it easily with thirty-nine seats to just ten for the carping CCF. Even "Honest Bob" Sommers, who should have stepped aside until the charges against him had been dealt with, was easily re-elected in Rossland-Trail. It was, said Bennett humbly, "the greatest victory for the ordinary people since the Magna Carta." The conspiracy by the city slickers against his little government had been crushed. The allegations against Sommers were mere "fluff, fluff and bluff," and Bonner was the greatest attorney-general the province had ever seen.

Not all his backbenchers agreed with this assessment. One of them, Mel Bryan, said Bonner should resign. He crossed the floor into the Opposition benches to back up his words. Bennett, the original floor-crosser who never dealt in personalities, branded Bryan a "traitor" and gratuitously accused him of packing a nomination meeting to get elected.

Eventually, three years after the original charges, Sommers was hauled into court, convicted of taking bribes and sentenced to five years in prison. Everybody else involved in the affair got off scot-free. Bennett and Bonner were never called to account for their deliberate suppression of the facts. And the principal firm involved, B.C. Forest Products, a part of the E.P. Taylor empire of Toronto, was also unscathed. As Socred backbencher Cyril Shelford wondered aloud, "how can Sommers be guilty of taking a bribe if no company gave him any money?"

There were many other unanswered questions. Sommers' defence counsel, Angelo Branca, the top criminal lawyer in the province, said he did not know at the time who paid his fees. Later he learned it was an unnamed prominent industrialist. Sommers' outstanding bank loan was said to have been paid off by Social Credit party funds controlled by Gunderson. And Bennett's crony Waldo Skillings was involved in some clandestine negotiations with Sommers in a Seattle motel, offering him $25,000 to stay out of the country. The money was said to have been put up by unidentified Vancouver businessmen.

The other cabinet member in and out of trouble throughout the Bennett era was Highways Minister Rev. P. A. "Flying Phil" Gaglardi. Gaglardi had a fondness for fast cars and Lear jets. The first cost him a number of speeding tickets; the second got him in hot water when he used the government aircraft to fly back and forth to his Kamloops Pentecostal church on weekends and to take relatives on a trip to the U.S. He gave no-bid contracts to Socred supporters, some of whom gratefully donated labour and materials to his church addition, and his two sons made fortunes speculating in land which happened to end up alongside new highways. "Just because their father was Highways Minister," Gaglardi said, "did that mean these boys had to be second-class citizens?" No indeed. They were "entitled to do what any other private citizen could do."

In 1960 Gaglardi was fined $1,000 for contempt of court after disregarding a court order to hold up department funds to a highway contractor during litigation. His stock answer was to blame his problems on a "conspiracy" that was out to get him as it had Sommers. Throughout it all Bennett remained loyal to his feisty little colleague. At times tears came to the Premier's eyes when Gaglardi launched into one of his bombastic flights of oratory in the legislature. Bennett accused the press of attacking Gaglardi "because he is a man of the cloth." ("I never criticize the press," Bennett once declared in a typical non sequitur. "I said they have a right to criticize me and I have the right to criticize them.")

• • •

Bennett's two-river policy and subsequent takeover of the B.C. Electric Company were brought on in part by his blunder in being taken in by a big-talking international development firm, the Axel Wenner-Gren interests of Sweden. In 1956 Bennett signed a memorandum-of-intent with the firm to develop 40,000 square miles of northeastern B.C., one-tenth of the province.

The cornerstone of the project was a 400-mile monorail along the Rocky Mountain trench going from nowhere to nowhere. Investment of $1 billion was suggested, in the days when a billion was still a lot of money. A similarly ambitious scheme in Southern Rhodesia had recently been abandoned by Wenner-Gren, but no matter. Bennett's northern development dream was in full flower. A place was found on the board of directors for Einar Gunderson. Profits were to be donated to scientific research. It sounded too good to be true, and it was.

Wenner-Gren spent a few thousand dollars on showy "surveys," got some world-wide publicity, then lost interest in the whole affair. Desperate to salvage something from the wreckage, Bennett came up with a plan to dam the mighty Peace River. He carried this vision into the 1960 election with yet another slogan, "Vote for the Government that gets things done." To make sure the public got the message, industrialist Frank McMahon warned just two days before the election that if the socialists won, $450 million in gas and oil investment would be lost to the province at a cost of 10,000 jobs. The Vancouver *Province* was pleased to run McMahon's concerns under a screaming front-page headline. The Socreds won thirty-two seats, down from thirty-nine but still a comfortable majority. Their share of the vote was thirty-nine per cent.

When CCF Leader Robert Strachan had called during the campaign for public ownership of the giant B.C. Electric Company, the Socreds scoffed at the notion. The *Province* called Strachan the "Fidel Castro of British Columbia" for thinking such a thing. Within a year Bennett's free enterprise government did it. There was a bit of a fuss but when Bennett upped the compensation for company shareholders following court action, the takeover was peacefully completed.

The government had become the biggest employer in the province. It ran a railway, a ferry fleet and delivered electricity and natural gas. All this expansion of the public sector required capital, but since Bennett had always boasted of the government's pay-as-you-go philosophy, it became necessary to disguise the borrowing. He did this by creative bookkeeping using "contingent liabilities" in which the debts of crown agencies were not recorded in the provincial budget. British Columbia was transformed into a fiscal fantasyland which some cynics likened to Social Credit's "funny money."

While Bennett bragged that B.C. was debt-free, the Dominion Bureau of Statistics showed that the province had the highest per capita debt in the country. The voters never really understood Bennett's financial shell game and didn't seem to care. They were easily bought off by minor cuts in nuisance taxes and fees, and grants to homeowners. Like the federal family allowance program, this was simply a case of bribing the people with their own money. The homeowner scheme was justified by Bennett on the grounds that "if we are to stop Socialism and Communism we must have owners of homes and farms." While preaching the virtues of capitalism, he was encouraging the people to rely on the government to promote their well-being.

As the years and the election victories (seven) rolled by, Bennett became puffed with power, increasingly self-satisfied and preachy. A cartoonist saw him as the ever-grinning Cheshire Cat. It was no longer the Social Credit government, but rather the Bennett government. Getting his picture on the cover of *Time* magazine in 1966 was a crowning glory. Who cared now if the sophisticates of Toronto regarded Bennett as a buffoon and B.C. politics as zany? Bennett thought big and his tenure coincided with a dramatic increase in the living standards of most British Columbians. With his slick team of public relations men selling the good life to the voters, he seemed invincible.

As Bennett rolled to his sixth win in 1966, federal NDP leader Tommy Douglas described the Socreds as "the most ruthless, arrogant, well-oiled, wealthiest political machine that ever existed in British Columbia." Douglas claimed Bennett wanted to wipe out the NDP as "the conscience of the government," but he was wrong about that. Bennett needed the NDP. Without it as a foil, there was no reason for Social Credit to exist.

On the heels of the province's first billion-dollar budget, Bennett went to the people again in 1969 and scored his biggest win ever, thirty-eight of fifty-five seats. One of his victims was the new

NDP leader, Tom Berger, who Bennett had labelled a "city slicker labour lawyer," which in Socred parlance was four epithets in a row. Berger was replaced by social worker Dave Barrett.

• • •

Slowly, over the next three years, the political climate of British Columbia underwent a change. The unemployment rate climbed to ten per cent. Productivity had increased in the resource industries but jobs were being lost to technological change. There was concern over rising inflation. Even more damaging to Social Credit was the admission of Robert Bonner when he left government for private business in 1968 that the party had oversold the idea of ever-increasing wealth. "There is a failure to relate our expectations with our capacities," Bonner said. "We have deluded ourselves into believing that there is some sort of magic in government financing."

But it was too late for Bennett to adjust to the changing times. He was a victim of his own malarkey, out of touch with new pressure groups concerned about pollution, preserving the environment, replanting the forests. As his government skidded in popularity Bennett could only rant against the forces of evil which were out to get "this little Social Credit government."

He called an election for August 30, 1972. Now almost seventy-two, Bennett had lost his zip. He campaigned only two or three hours a day in a three-day campaign week. There was no spontaneity and little contact with the public. He was preaching only to the converted, not reaching out to the uncommitted as he had done in seven previous elections. He focussed on the past rather than the future, showing a film entitled "Twenty Great Years." He told the voters that the only issue "is whether you want to be on the opposition side or the government side." The old cry that "The Socialist hordes are at the gates" didn't frighten the people as it had in past times. The only issue now was the Premier himself and whether he was still able to lead the province.

The answer was made clear when the votes were counted. Social Credit was decimated, winning only ten seats while the NDP took thirty-eight. There were five Liberals and two

Conservatives. Bennett held on to his South Okanagan seat, but it was small consolation. Eleven of his cabinet ministers went under. A relatively small switch of votes had resulted in a massive electoral change.

Perhaps because he had so little experience of it since 1952, Bennett turned out to be an ungracious loser. "I am a poor politician because I did not try to please all the people all the time," he said with pseudo humility. He blamed his defeat on the press and militant school teachers, and even the big money interests angered by his ban on liquor and tobacco advertisements.

But when all was said and rationalized, it boiled down to the fact that the aged slugger had not known when to hang up his gloves. Wacky Bennett had simply overstayed his time in the premier's office.

William Vander Zalm

Chapter 7.

The Fantasy Man

Not only had W. A. C. Bennett failed to exit before the inevitable defeat of age, he had refused to groom a successor or even think about the possibility of being replaced. It had been assumed by some that Robert Bonner was the man who would take over. Cool and intelligent, Bonner was the only cabinet minister who had Bennett's confidence. But perhaps Bennett realized that the stiff-necked lawyer was not a man of the people and lacked the instincts of a successful politician. Because the leadership was never held out to him, the Attorney-General resigned after sixteen years of faithful service.

There was also the Gaglardi factor. The only cabinet minister openly ambitious to succeed Bennett, the bombastic little preacher knew he was popular with the grass-roots of the party. The Premier responded by putting him in charge of the welfare ministry, a likely graveyard for anyone aspiring to the top job. Gaglardi later raised eyebrows in the 1972 campaign when he described his cabinet colleagues as square pegs in round holes and said Bennett was an old man who no longer understood the young. "I'm the only real choice for the job," he added modestly. Gaglardi's antics didn't help Bennett hang on to power.

It has been suggested that Bennett was thinking of stepping down in 1970 but decided against it because he feared Gaglardi would win a leadership fight. It seems unlikely, however, that Bennett ever seriously considered retiring. After the election defeat one of his best and most loyal cabinet ministers, Ray Williston, was critical: "I think he should have stepped down halfway in the term before and let somebody become established as leader for a brief period and then let the people decide. People didn't have confidence that he was going to be there for any period of time."

• • •

Meanwhile, jovial Dave Barrett had taken over the premier's office with little preparation or thought about how to organize and run a government. He left the cabinet structure much as it had been under Bennett, but it was soon apparent that he lacked the authority to make it run smoothly. Unlike Bennett, Barrett was fraternal rather than paternal, which may make for a more likeable man but in political leaders usually results in chaotic government.

But Barrett wasn't all smiles 'n chuckles. He had a darker side. Touchy about criticism, he carried on a running war with the press. There was also a vindictiveness which showed in his unwillingness to forgive those party members who had supported Tom Berger against him in the 1969 leadership convention. The contest followed the resignation of Bob Strachan, another frustrated Bennett victim.

Barrett emulated Wacky Bennett more than his son Bill did, even in his language. Barrett put down the Liberal turncoats as "city slicker lawyers." He was strongly partisan and relished scoring petty one-upmanship victories over his political foes. There was little effort to defuse the polarization which had gripped the province for the past two decades. Barrett was a war history buff and looked on the Legislature as a battlefield much as his predecessor had done.

Policy initiatives — there were some good ones — usually came from the most forceful cabinet minister, Bob Williams. With his low threshold of boredom and lack of tolerance for those he considered less bright than himself (which included all reporters and most of his colleagues), Williams alienated many with his arrogance.

Cabinet posts had been given only to those MLAs who had sat in Opposition, which meant there were no fresh faces or ideas. The old gang had just moved across the aisle into the government benches. Research and support staff were skimpy. Legislation was often badly drafted and there was much bungling and backtracking. Coordination between government departments and agencies was almost non-existent. The caucus had little input on policy, which in the absence of an overall blueprint appeared to be scattergun, sprung on the public without advance preparation. And despite talk of a more open government, there was an almost paranoiac concern for secrecy.

The government's problems were compounded by the expectations of unionized workers who had waited so long for a sympathetic government. When Barrett did not meet the hefty contract demands of ferry workers and staff of the new automobile Insurance Corporation of B.C., they went out on strike. The public bore the brunt of the walkout and the government, caught in a double bind, eventually caved in to the workers to get them back to work. Those settlements set wage demands spiralling in the rest of the economy.

Barrett lacked Bennett's expertise as finance minister, and did little or nothing to put an end to Bennett's debt manipulation accounting. For a time it didn't matter. The Treasury was loaded. "Money seemed to be coming off the trees," said one political scientist. The economy was booming and resource revenues were pouring into the Treasury. There seemed no need to establish priorities or spending guidelines. The advice of bureaucratic experts and academics was mistrusted.

When the resource-based economy inevitably went into one of its cyclical downslides, the government appeared to have been caught offguard. While Bennett had shrewdly underestimated revenues to come up with budget surpluses, Barrett underestimated expenditures. This misjudgement was compounded by the revelation of huge cost-overruns by individual departments, resulting in a public perception of financial and administrative incompetence. Throughout, Barrett appeared too casual about it all, carried away by misplaced confidence in his political astuteness. He had ignored the wishes of the grassroots and angered party purists by not implementing all they had been demanding for years and now unrealistically believed could be introduced immediately. The growing sense of dissatisfaction with the government was reflected in the federal election in the summer of 1975 when the NDP dropped nine of its eleven seats in the province.

• • •

It should have been easy for the Barrett government. The opposition was in disarray. Wacky Bennett was officially the Leader of the Opposition but had no zest for the job. After announcing that he intended to step down as party leader and resign his seat, Bennett and his wife took off on his first real vacation since entering politics. Belatedly attempting to pass his mantle to Leslie Peterson, who had succeeded Bonner as attorney-general, he gave the job of reorganizing the party to former cabinet ministers Grace McCarthy and Dan Campbell. McCarthy was bitter after the loss of her own seat to the NDP. She blamed the Liberals and Tories for splitting the free enterprise vote. Her successful crusade to rebuild Social Credit was motivated partly by a desire to keep the old-line parties in the political wilderness.

While Social Credit was attempting to re-establish itself, there was a move to create a new Unity Party or Majority Movement to take its place as the conservative alternative to socialism. For a time it appeared that the Socred coalition might come apart. But then Bill Bennett decided to enter the fray and launch a Bennett Socred dynasty. Bennett Jr. began by winning the Okanagan byelection opened up by his father's resignation, then in November of 1973 was the overwhelming choice of the party as leader.

With McCarthy diligently signing up new members, Bill Bennett set out to head off the threat of a new party filling the vacuum on the right. In many ways he seemed the wrong man for the task. It is difficult to understand what motivated Bill Bennett. He lacked the zest of his father for political combat and was uncomfortable and inarticulate on a stage or before a battery of microphones and television cameras. The glare of publicity made him cringe. Unlike his father, he was shy and a poor salesman. On television he was wooden. Bill's off-the-cuff answers to reporters' questions were often incomprehensible. Newsmen busily writing or listening to tapes afterward found he had made little or no sense. At times it seemed he had inherited only his father's garbled syntax.

A newspaper columnist wrote after an interview with Bill Bennett that "answers seem to slide off into digressive word jungles rooted in a welter of statistics." Like his father he couldn't deal "with any dimension beyond the material." This was not surprising, since he had grown up with the hardware business and his father's superficial brand of politics as his only realities.

Bill Bennett later claimed he had "wanted to work, to win, to help take some of the sting out of the defeat my father had suffered. This was the most powerful motive in the world." There is no doubt the Bennett clan was badly shaken by the 1972 election, but it is an unconvincing explanation. Bill Bennett was clearly driven by some deeper force to prove that he was his own man. His father had been too busy to be close to his two sons, and when Bill became leader he pushed his father roughly aside, even though the old man felt he still had something to contribute. The son was determined to recast the party with a more youthful image. He allied himself with big business and Howe Street more than his father ever had.

With the help of some political technocrats hired in

Ontario, Bennett succeeded despite all his handicaps in rebuilding the party. The remnants of the Majority Movement had no option but to jump on the Social Credit bandwagon. Tories Hugh Curtis and Peter Hyndman and political chameleon Bill Vander Zalm came over in 1974. They were followed a year later by Liberals Pat McGeer, Allan Williams and Garde Gardom. Bill Bennett explained their conversions thus: "In business, when you want to expand, you use one company as a vehicle. You naturally choose the one with the broadest bases and the best-known name." It was a revealing view of his perception of politics.

When the general election was called for December 11, 1975, Bennett was ready. Barrett, who had been critical of Wacky Bennett for calling elections every three years, had hoped to catch the Socreds and their new leader off-guard by going to the people with twenty months of the government's mandate still remaining. He had been pushed by Bob Williams but opposed by a number of ministers and caucus members who feared defeat. (Barrett was also going against party policy in other provinces where NDP premiers, led by Tommy Douglas in Saskatchewan for twenty years, pledged in advance to hold elections in June every four years.) Barrett confidently told the caucus he would resign as leader if the government lost, but hung around for another ten years anyway.

The public was dissatisfied with the performance of the NDP. A bloated civil service had increased by almost a third in only three years and salaries and benefits had soared. Barrett attempted to joke his way through the campaign and his personality rather than policies became the issue. Even party supporters considered him to be too clownish and patronizing. The socialists were ripe for plucking and the opposition was now solidly Social Credit once again. The conservatives were brought on side by that old-time fear of socialism rather than any promise of new policies or even a return to the good old days of dear old Dad. Social Credit took almost fifty per cent of the vote and elected thirty-five members, to only eighteen for the NDP. The Liberal and Conservative remnants came up with one seat each. In the end nothing became Dave Barrett so much as his concession speech, which was gracious and good-humoured, an object lesson for all politicians who go down to defeat and bitterly blame everybody but themselves.

● ● ●

Bill Bennett now went to work as premier in a far different manner than his father. This was a cold, bloodless administration reflecting the personality of the boss. Populism was out; the dispassionate expertise of political science was in. Cabinet ministers were kept under a tight rein, acting or speaking only with the approval of the premier's office. Routine departmental press releases were bloated with political puffery. Bennett and his advisers became obsessed with opinion polls. The government made few moves without reading the pollsters' teacups.

Bennett Sr. had shifted power from the legislature to the cabinet room; Bennett Jr. now proceeded to consolidate it in the premier's office. It was there that aggressive fund-raising in the boardrooms was organized. Social Credit became the open party of big business and the far right. W.A.C. Bennett had always denied the connection, but now there was no question. Anti-union legislation was introduced and outside investment encouraged in the resource industries.

"He's a businessman's businessman," said tycoon Jimmy Pattison approvingly. "The positive side about Bill Bennett is that he really cares about money." That attitude inevitably brought him close to the Howe Street gonzos who donated generously to the party coffers. "I've never seen the street get together on anything like this before," said stock promoter Murray Pezim, who estimated the total at $1 million for the 1983 campaign. Bennett won the support of the Vancouver Stock Exchange boys by declaring that "economic development is the only social policy." Welfare and education funding was lower on the Social Credit priority list than ever before. The new doctrines were handed down from the economic panjandrums of the far-right Fraser Institute.

Bennett bravely proclaimed that "B.C. is not for sale"

and blocked the sale of forestry giant MacMillan Bloedel to the CPR. Not long after, however, when the Eastern conglomerate Noranda took over MacBlo he didn't utter a murmur of protest. There were numerous other sales to outsiders, especially in the coal-mining industry which Bennett was anxious to promote. Once again the emphasis was placed on exploitation of resources.

The government borrowed enormous sums of money for railroads and shipping facilities to open up coal fields for the Japanese market. The investment proved disastrous when world coal prices dipped and long-term contracts were renogotiated. The open-pit mining operations were unpopular with environmentalists and created few jobs.

There were other projects conceived on the grand scale, such as a new high-speed highway to the interior of the province, development of Vancouver's False Creek in advance of Expo 86, including construction of a costly covered stadium for professional sports. Journalists gibed that Bill had inherited his father's "edifice complex." When he attempted a political gimmick like Bennett Sr.'s homeowner grant, Bill Bennett fell on his face. Such was the case with the infamous British Columbia Resources Investment Corporation, or BCRIC for short.

The acronym was apt, since the shares in government-owned industries, most of them acquired during the NDP regime, soon became a political brick tied to the Premier's neck. The idea behind it all was to "privatize" the businesses and get the public involved in speculative investment. Five shares valued at about $6 each were handed out to every adult citizen in the province and the public was urged to buy more on the open market. Many did, believing that any stock backed by the government would not be allowed to fail. It seemed like a sure thing. The value of the shares did shoot up for a time to around $9, but then began a slow but steady slide to well under $1. There was much bickering over management of the corporation, from which Bennett desperately attempted to distance himself.

At the same time as Bennett was throwing money at his prized mega-projects, he embarked on a ballyhooed but selective program of restraint in the public sector. As Marjorie Nichols, the most astute political columnist in B.C., saw it, "Bill Bennett wanted to strip things from those people who, from his small-town businessman's point of view, weren't producing: welfare recipients, the elderly and those with no real gumption." These presumably included university students, lazy schoolteachers and civil servants. (All this while some of his fat cat cabinet ministers were putting New York theatres, upscale hotels, limousines, prostitutes and Pouilly-Fuisse wine on their expense account credit cards.)

Despite the scandals, and in the face of determined opposition from the teachers and labour unions, Bennett surprised almost everyone by easily winning general elections in 1979 and 1983. He succeeded in large part by following his image-makers' advice to become a "tough guy" ready to lead the province through hard times. Government "restraint" and wage controls were the causes of the day. Dave Barrett, who had tried in vain to persuade the voters that he was a new and different man than the premier they remembered from 1972 to 1975, finally gave up. He was succeeded by the lacklustre Bob Skelly, who was in turn followed by the ineffective Mike Harcourt.

With his 1979 mandate, Bennett pushed ahead with pet projects, particularly Expo, which was to become a great success despite dire predictions. He became an increasingly isolated figure, however, living alone in a Victoria hotel suite with little public contact. He had few friends among his colleagues and was most compatible with Vancouver's financial wheelers and dealers. Like his father, he believed that loneliness went with leadership.

It was this attitude that partly explained Bennett's sudden, odd departure from politics in May of 1986. His popularity had been slipping in his beloved polls, which showed him running behind the party, but nobody anticipated his resignation. "My father stayed too long," he said simply. The party needed renewal, Bennet declared, but like his father he had groomed no successor. Bennett said the new leader should be picked by a party convention rather than himself or the caucus.

The leave-taking was without apparent emotion. One of his aides was delegated to notify the stunned cabinet. Bennett had lunch with a group of businessmen who had contributed large sums to his political fund. "These were the guys he was comfortable with," an aide said. Some speculated that he had decided to quit after the opening of the Coquihalla Highway, which he indicated was the summit of his ten-year political career. "Now I can die happy," he had said at the opening day ceremony. (Later it was revealed that the highway budget had gone far over estimates because of his unrealistic orders that it be completed in time for the Expo opening, but Bennett was never called to account). Whatever his reasoning, it was a cold, calculated move that mirrored the man. And whatever the motive for this non-political man to enter politics, he had apparently proved something to himself.

Not even Audrey Bennett was quite sure what motivated her husband. "He had a mission in life," she told an interviewer, "but I never thought it would be political." His goal was to make $1 million before he was thirty, she said. (Audrey said she didn't know whether he had made it, which says a lot about the separation of powers in the households of W. A.C. Bennett and Bill.)

Audrey said Bill was bored with his business affairs and needed a challenge, which presented itself in politics. She protested his decision to follow in his father's footsteps, but in vain. Like her mother-in-law, she was left to bring up the children virtually alone. Audrey also regretted the change of personality which public life caused in her husband. He was no longer able to relax socially and always seemed to have his guard up. He became increasingly aloof and isolated, except when he returned to his home and friends in Kelowna.

Bill Bennett is a compulsive man who compartmentalizes his life. He was obsessed with making it on his own, even though his father gave him a head start in both business and politics. That can lead to a sense of resentment in a determined young man. Bill Bennett seemed to be displaying that when he deliberately kept his distance from his father through the leadership campaign, and during his time in office while Bennett Sr. was still alive.

His aides claimed that Bennett had sacrificed himself in the interests of preserving the party. Such high-mindedness is rare enough in any political party; for Social Credit it is unimaginable. In the event, Bennett succeeded instead in splitting the party, perhaps irreparably. One hesitates to guess about the shadowy side of Bill Bennett's psyche, but it is hard to escape the conclusion that even with his limited grasp of politics, he must have foreseen what would happen in the rush to fill the vacancy he had created.

Bill had taken the loose amalgam created by his father and guided and transformed it into the semblance of a high-tech, strategizing modern political party. The populist old guard of Social Credit reluctantly accepted the new approach as long as it could deliver the goods on election day. Now they were being given an unexpected opportunity to regain control of the party as they once knew it. There is no small irony in the fact that they represented the traditions of Wacky Bennett, who had died in 1979, while his son's followers were headed in another direction. The odd relationship between father and son was brought into the open one last time.

Bennett's choice as his successor was Bud Smith, a bright young Kamloops lawyer hired by the Premier as his principal secretary after Smith orchestrated a surprising Socred byelection victory in his area in 1981. Smith had never held any elected office, but Bennett pointed out that neither had he when he went after the leadership.

Members of the cabinet naturally resented this attempted anointing, seeing it as an attempt by non-elected appointees in the premier's office to control the party's destiny. Four of them entered the leadership race, as well as three MLAs and five outsiders, including Bud Smith and Bill Vander Zalm, who had been on the sidelines since 1983.

Vander Zalm was the last to throw his hat in the ring. He was concerned about a shaky $10 million dollar investment in Fantasy Garden World, his biblical theme park in suburban Vancouver. But he was an ambitious man who found it hard to resist the pressure from a number of quarters to join the fray. Like

Phil Gaglardi of an earlier era, he was immensely popular among the rank-and-file party members. (Gaglardi later endorsed him in the leadership contest because he was the only candidate with "guts"). Even Grace McCarthy, a rival for that constituency, urged Vander Zalm to run. McCarthy was particularly outspoken about Bennett's leadership, saying he had adopted all the worst features of the Ontario Tory machine, whose operatives he had hired. It was perhaps a herald of things to come that the Conservatives had just been tossed out of office in Ontario.

• • •

Except for the fact that he began in municipal politics and was involved with the Liberals instead of the Tories, Vander Zalm's zig-zag path to the leadership convention had some striking similarities to that taken by W. A. C. Bennett. After serving as an alderman and then mayor for six years in Surrey, Vander Zalm ran as a Liberal candidate in a federal general election and lost. Four years later he had shifted to the provincial scene and failed in a bid for the Liberal leadership. He turned next to Social Credit. Soon after joining he tried to get the Socreds to change their name to the "B.C. Party," which would at least have recognized its true coalition character, but found little support. That issue forgotten, Vander Zalm was elected to the Legislature in 1976.

Although his charismatic style did not fit into the Bill Bennett system, he was given three tough cabinet portfolios over the next seven years: Municipal Affairs, Education, and Human Resources. While always controversial with his shoot-from-the-lip remarks, Vander Zalm was generally regarded as a capable administrator. (As Marjorie Nichols noted, he "performs well on a leash controlled by someone else ... but left to his own devices runs out of control.") He often rankled his cabinet colleagues, and after they refused to support a land use measure he had sponsored, Vander Zalm abruptly resigned after calling them "gutless." He also took a jab at Bennett's leadership by complaining that his office staff were wielding too much power.

It was a criticism that would come back to haunt him when the same charge was later made against him as premier.

Some party officials never forgave Vander Zalm for stepping aside at that time, knowing that the Socreds were facing a tough election battle. It was widely regarded as an opportunistic move designed to help him get the leadership sometime in the future. His prospects did not look promising, however, after making an ill-considered bid for the Vancouver mayoralty. He ran a bad race, indulging in red-baiting against NDP incumbent Mike Harcourt and left-wing members of the City Council. Harcourt won easily. The joy of victory, however, was relatively short-lived. A few years later he would find himself playing second fiddle to Vander Zalm in the legislature.

In 1979 Vander Zalm had denied wanting the Socred leadership, "but eight or ten years down the road if I'm still interested and if the people still want me, then maybe I'll take a shot at it."

● ● ●

The leadership convention, only the second in the party's thirty-four-year history, was held in the expensive, trendy resort town of Whistler. Despite all the backstage power struggles, in the end the race came down to a personality contest. That kind of competition gave Vander Zalm and his legendary charm the upper hand. The polls showed that he was by far the most popular candidate with the public, and the Socreds above all wanted to pick a leader who could win an election.

A lot of money was spent at Whistler wining and dining the delegates, but Vander Zalm ran the stingiest campaign of all. While the other leading candidates leaned on the high-priced advice of hired guns, he ran his own show. There was no communication with the other camps; no deals cut or fancy strategies plotted. Vander Zalm did not have the support of any cabinet ministers and maverick millionaire Edgar Kaiser was the only prominent businessman who supported him.

Bill and his wife Lillian simply did a royal walkabout

through the streets of the town each evening, flashing smiles and small talk. (One of the sore losers, Health Minister Jim Nielsen, said later that B.C. had wanted a Prince Charles and Diana pair and got it in Bill and Lil.)

But the coronation was not quite automatic. On July 30 the balloting went down to a final shoot-out between Vander Zalm and Attorney-General Brian Smith. Vander Zalm won handily, despite the fact that half the delegates were federal Tories, and natural allies of Smith. Vander Zalm was the only candidate who had drawn votes from all regions of the province. Grace McCarthy had been the last candidate knocked out and most of her delegates had gone over to him. "I was very relieved that it turned out the way it did," McCarthy said, "because I felt it was in the right hands at the right time in the province's history." She compared Vander Zalm's populism with that of W.A.C. Bennett and welcomed the "fresh new approach."

In the final ballot Vander Zalm and Smith represented the two wings of the Social Credit party, the mavericks and the establishment. Marjorie Nichols wrote: "The neo-conservative Social Credit machine built by Bill Bennett is dead, the victim of a freakish head-on collision with a grassroots bulldozer driven by an unelected rampaging populist." Vander Zalm, the man who wanted to give a shovel to able-bodied welfare recipients and had made it his symbol, said it was "the triumph of the shovel over the machine."

Seven days later Vander Zalm was sworn in as premier. After only six weeks in office he called an election for October 22. The result was almost a foregone conclusion. The electoral map had been redrawn with the addition of twelve seats, all but one in Social Credit strongholds. NDP leader Bob Skelly was stricken by nerves when faced by cameras and microphones during the campaign and was unable to inspire public confidence. Vander Zalm had virtually no policy or platform, simply promising more consultation and less confrontation with special interest groups. He seemed to be running more against the Bill Bennett record than the NDP. The salesman was selling himself. Just give me a chance, he asked the voters, as Wacky had done thirty-four years before. They did, emphatically, handing Vander Zalm forty-seven of the sixty-nine seats. The shattered NDP got the other twenty-two.

It was a one-man victory. British Columbia had been given a choice, and as it had so many times in the past, picked the most colourful, unpredictable candidate. Vander Zalm was more the successor of Wacky Bennett than he was of Bill Bennett. He was perceived as a return to the charismatic salesman for the province and its resource riches.

• • •

Now it only remained to see what kind of premier Vander Zalm would turn out to be. There were plenty of clues in his background.

For five years during the Second World War, from age five to ten, Vander Zalm had been brought up by his mother under great hardships in ravaged Holland. His father was in Canada on a bulb-selling trip when war broke out and remained here for the duration, building up an extensive business in the Fraser Valley. Jovial and gregarious, Vander Zalm Sr. had a reputation as a sharp businessman.

When the family was reunited here after the war, young Bill had decided he wanted to become a lawyer but was forced to take over the bulb business when his father died. With his father's gift of the gab, Bill began wooing the public by auctioning bulbs from the back of a truck in shopping centres. While on a selling trip to Kelowna the handsome young salesman discovered Lillian, who worked as a waitress by day and sold candy in the movie theatre lobby at night. "As soon as I saw him I knew he was the one," Lillian gushed. "He was just my type, clean, smiling and cheeky."

Vander Zalm was also a hard worker and was soon looking for ways to expand his growing nursery business. He found the capital by dealing in property and stretching local zoning laws to their limits. A familiar tactic was to violate the code, then appeal to the municipal council that it would be unfair to undo his investment. Like Wacky Bennett he was optimistic, tenacious and had a sharp business eye. And he brought some of

Wacky's skills to politics. "Politics is marketing," Vander Zalm once declared. Like Bennett, he is pragmatic and non-ideological, believing only that if you haven't made it in the world then you haven't really tried. By working hard as he had done, a man could achieve anything.

Carried to its extreme, this simplistic philosophy leads to a belief in one's infallibility. "Untroubled by self-doubt, he is the master of easy answers," a reporter wrote of Vander Zalm. Whatever he does or says must be right. Anyone who questions his views or methods is simply misguided. He is sealed off from the real world by a web of fantasy. His critics can never reach him at the centre. Self-righteousness reigns supreme. In his case the line between praiseworthy determination and dogged stubbornness is almost invisible.

While mayor of Surrey for six years, Vander Zalm preached the gospel of teamwork and openness but created mistrust and divisiveness. He claimed to be a liberal but brought in redneck policies. (When he later sought the Liberal leadership Vander Zalm said he would lash drug pushers and cut off "welfare deadbeats.") While others on Council were accused of violating conflict of interest rules, he skated close to the edge of that slippery pond but never fell in.

Vander Zalm took pride in the fact that he was a man in a hurry: "I can't stand waiting about." He had no time for committees, in-depth reviews or bureaucrats in general. Hassled by provincial marketing boards when he tried to sell lettuce from his farmlands, Vander Zalm began trucking his produce to Seattle. Farmers and small businessmen identify with his frustrations, which are magnified at the local level. The problems become far more complex at the provincial level, however.

Vander Zalm is not consistent even on this issue, supposedly the one dearest to his political heart. "I hate bureaucracy," he declares emphatically. "We've got too many rules that make it hard for you to do your job." Yet in office he has tended to exercise tight control over business development. "My argument is that individuals sometimes have to give up their rights for the over-all good of the community," Vander Zalm says in his defence. But the problem, once again, is that it's *his* idea of what's good for the community that prevails.

In office, however, Vander Zalm does not care to admit there is such a thing as a problem. "Whatever happens was meant to be," he says, which would seem to absolve a political leader of blame for just about anything that happens under his jurisdiction. "You get your setbacks and you get your hurts," he says, "but if you accept them and push on and do what you believe to be right, it will turn out the way it's supposed to in the end."

In March of 1986 Vander Zalm said the recession of the early 1980s in B.C. had been a good thing. It enabled people to appreciate good times when they returned. "I think God sent it. It was needed." There's a kind of mystic fatalism in this attitude and, sure enough, Vander Zalm, a devout Roman Catholic, is able to incorporate this kind of thinking into his beliefs. He is intrigued by numerology and extrasensory perception.

"This is all governed by someone else," he says. "We're just players in the game." There's more of this ethereal philosophy: "If a person does his or her very best, with good intentions, fairly and truthfully, then the result — whatever it is — was meant to be." That's reminiscent of Phil Gaglardi's memorable line that "if I tell a lie it's only because I believe I'm telling the truth." In short, they can do no wrong. That's a dangerous attitude in any politician, but especially in one who believes in little except himself.

It is not surprising that a man with Vander Zalm's classic good looks would be narcissistic. The easy-mannered charm is as carefully cultivated and groomed as the picture-perfect clothes. The matter of Vander Zalm's style arose at Whistler when leadership candidate Kim Campbell said of him that "charisma without substance is a dangerous thing." Vander Zalm responded that style *is* substance. Substance without style gets you nowhere. "Where you can beat your competition is in style," he said, adding with mangled grammar and typical shallowness: "Do it classy."

Vander Zalm says W.A.C. Bennett always advised him to keep his political horse in the middle of the road, away from the right side. Ignoring the advice, he has consistently disdained moderation and galloped off to join British Columbia's notoriously long line of extremists. (Wacky himself zig-zagged so wildly from side to side down the political road that he was hardly in a position to preach moderation to anyone.) "I like to say what I am thinking," Vander Zalm declares, and it is these off-the-cuff opinions that inevitably get him in hot water, which he at times appears to enjoy. He has a gift for coming up with the headline-grabbing phrase and takes a perverse enjoyment in being outrageous.

Vander Zalm has an instinctive shrewdness. He is adept at fielding questions from the media pack, taking time to look for the trap before giving an answer. Where Bill Bennett smiled wanly and ran for cover, and his father merely smiled, Vander Zalm stands up to rigorous cross-examination by the press. That at least, is a refreshing change. He is unusually forthright and candid for a politician. And he is less partisan than Dave Barrett or the Bennetts. In the legislature his style is soft rather than belligerent. Questions are answered with vague and uncertain musings. Vander Zalm's instincts are not those of a politician, and that will probably be his undoing. (That and the fact that as Vancouver *Sun* columnist Vaughan Palmer has noted, Vander Zalm is "vulnerable to ridicule, as only a politician who lives in a castle can be.")

● ● ●

On the night of his 1986 election victory Vander Zalm let it be known that the premier's office would play a stronger role in governing the province. It marked an abrupt about-turn from his earlier criticism of Bill Bennett's administration. It was not realized at the time what sweeping changes were in store. The man who had promised more public participation in government and less red-tape, proceeded to take the opposite tack.

The staff of the premier's office was bumped from thirteen under Bill Bennett to eighty-eight, with an annual budget of close to $7 million. Power was further centralized by having deputy ministers reporting to to the Premier through his appointed aides rather than to their own ministers. Although he campaigned against Bill Bennett's style of government, Vander Zalm believes like both Bennetts that cabinet ministers are relatively unimportant in the scheme of things. And so he appropriated the formation of policy to himself, confirming in the public's mind the perception that he was running an old style one-man government.

Then, in the name of decentralization, Vander Zalm announced his intention — without first consulting or even advising the caucus — to divide the province into eight regions, thereby creating a new level of government. The cabinet ministers named to head up the regional apparatus also reported to the premier's office. Creation of regional economic zones and planning guidelines was part of a 1981 Land Use Act which Vander Zalm attempted to introduce as Minister of Municipal Affairs under Bill Bennett. Bennett and some other cabinet ministers considered the measure a hot political potato and let it die on the order paper. It was that action that prompted Vander Zalm, urged on by Grace McCarthy, to call his colleagues gutless and leave Victoria for a time.

The Union of B.C. Municipalities had opposed the bill because it took power away from local regional boards. Vander Zalm's system would have the big decisions made under his aegis, a disguised form of centralization.

Accompanying the introduction of regions was the government's declaration that it intended to sell off a number of crown corporations and even sections of the civil service. Privatization, the buzzword made fashionable by Margaret Thatcher, had come to British Columbia with a vengeance. Vander Zalm had merely picked up the idea without any thought as to how it should be applied here. To many, it seemed like change for the sake of change with benefits only for the privateers.

Although he had campaigned on a promise to avoid the confrontations that marked the Bill Bennett administration, Vander Zalm seemed hell-bent in his first year as premier to embroil himself in contentious issues. The most bitter involved Bill 19, which drastically revised the provincial labour code.

Hastily written and requiring considerable revision, it pleased neither labour nor management. A companion piece of legislation, Bill 20, which reduced teachers' bargaining rights, met similar opposition. During debate on the two measures, opinion polls showed Vander Zalm's standing with the public was rapidly declining, but he pushed doggedly ahead.

Organized by the teachers and unions, a one-day general strike was held on June 1, 1987, in which an estimated 300,000 workers, or one-quarter of the province's labour force, stayed off the job, shutting down transportation and other services. Although the walkout was remarkably peaceful, Attorney-General Brian Smith rushed into court seeking an injunction against further strikes on the grounds that they amounted to sedition against the government. The application alleged there was a conspiracy to subvert the government by force, a preposterous claim thrown out by the court. Even the editorial writers of newspapers silenced by the strike later accused Smith and Vander Zalm of using a sledgehammer on legitimate protest, likening the government's action to the imposition of martial law in Poland. The goodwill which Vander Zalm had earned by averting a civil service strike soon after taking office had quickly evaporated.

• • •

Despite all these gaffes, and further allegations of conflict of interest by the Premier in attempting to advance the interests of his business partner Peter Toigo, it can be argued that Vander Zalm has not had a fair shake from the media. Reporters and columnists were at first delighted to have a premier who did not try to run away from their questions. On the anniversary of his first year in office in August of 1987 Vaughan Palmer praised Vander Zalm for conducting a government "more open, more accessible, more flexible than its predecessor." But Palmer and others who had treated Bill Bennett with kid gloves, turned on Vander Zalm with unparalleled fury when the mistakes began. Newsmen who have granted "honeymoons" to fresh-faced politicians like Brian Mulroney, Pierre Trudeau and Vander

Zalm, tend to act like spurned lovers when the affair ends. One rookie columnist with little apparent knowledge of politics or appreciation for democracy, stamped her feet and petulantly demanded that the Premier bow to her whims by resigning.

The conduct of some of his press gallery colleagues was questioned by freelance columnist Hubert Beyer, who wrote that there was an apparent witch-hunt against Vander Zalm. "There's a difference between rational criticism, no matter how stinging, and persecution," Beyer wrote. The media was leading the chorus to discredit the Premier, not just reporting it, he said. Questions were fired at Vander Zalm in the manner of an inquisition rather than a press conference, and undeserved praise was lavished on cabinet ministers such as Brian Smith and Grace McCarthy who broke with him for one reason or another. (A shakeout of the Whistler leadership contenders was inevitable at some time during Vander Zalm's administration.) In the long run Vander Zalm could be the beneficiary of public sympathy if the press continues its course of critical overkill.

Vander Zalm, like Ronald Reagan, has no time or patience for the details of governing. Both men act intuitively rather than on the basis of analysis. They prefer speaking platform platitudes to hammering out policy at the cabinet table. Neither likes to hear conflicting advice. Reagan mixed up the movies with real life while Vander Zalm confuses it with his private fantasy world. Both were elected partly because they gave the promise of escape from the world's cares and problems.

A bizarre example of Vander Zalm's dream world is his involvement in a Canadian made-for-TV movie entitled "Sinterklaas Fantasy." Sinterklaas is the 14th century patron saint of merchants and sailors in Holland and a sort of Santa Claus to children.

Semi-autobiographical, with Vander Zalm as narrator, the film tells the story of a little boy who comes to Canada from Holland. Later, grown into handsome manhood, he wanders through a garden daydreaming about his youth and the Dutch Santa Claus. A chance to return comes when Sinterklaas, who lives in a crystal palace in Spain, runs out of goodies to give away and sends a message to Fantasy Gardens asking for help. Santa Claus II is transported back to Holland via a magical frozen rainbow to become the Sinterklaas of his dreams, sailing on a canal boat and riding around the country on a white horse distributing presents. One need not make too much of the symbolism of the knight on the white horse, but it is little wonder that columnist Denny Boyd delights in calling Vander Zalm "The Wiz." (It is easier, however, to imagine Vander Zalm as the patient, good-natured father of a Hollywood sitcom family.) Sinterklaas was completed in December of 1987 after two years of "off-and-on" shooting and scheduled for future Christmas viewing.

• • •

Vander Zalm seems unaware that thinking out loud can get a political leader in a lot of trouble. The media lap these comments up. Every remark, no matter how offhand, is reported and magnified. Such was the case when he mused that the British parliamentary system is outdated because there is not enough public participation. Switzerland's use of referendums was preferable. Vander Zalm said that if he was a taxpayer in Richmond, he would want a vote on School District spending. In this instance he was ignoring recent provincial history. School Board referendums were dispensed with when it was found that people seldom if ever vote for an increase in taxes no matter how pressing the need. Governments themselves must accept the responsibility for funding essential services.

Most of his gaffes have been more spectacular. Not long after the election he met with South African ambassador Glenn Babb, a skilled advocate for the indefensible cause of Apartheid. Vander Zalm then announced that he was in favour of trade with South Africa, ignoring the fact that Canadian policy on the issue had already been decided by Ottawa. He was forced to back down, but the incident served to confirm the opinion of a former cabinet minister, since demoted, that "so much of his policy is the very last thing that anybody said to him. There is just no consistency."

Another more controversial issue, abortion, got Vander Zalm into even deeper trouble. This time the cause was his

162

inflexible moral code. Whatever he believes must be right for everyone else. Vander Zalm summed up his view of politics in a statement to the Socred caucus during the abortion dispute: "When you have a philosophy, when you have a set of principles by which you live and upon which you can depend and which the party can run with, when you have principles, you don't have to have consultants, you don't have to have big meetings to tell you what it is that needs doing." Those remarks confirm a critic's view that Vander Zalm's morality is "unresponsive to the tempering influence of the population around him."

When the Supreme Court of Canada ruled in effect that abortions were legal under any circumstances, Vander Zalm set out to defy the law of the land. He would refuse to provide government funding for abortions through the universal medical services health plan. A majority of the public was outraged. Again Vander Zalm was compelled to back down, but only after the B.C. Supreme Court ruled that he had no choice in the matter without bringing in special legislation.

Critics noted that while Vander Zalm regarded the fetus as sacred, his policies did not show the same regard for children. Undernourished pupils were denied school lunches on the spurious grounds that their parents, or parent, did not have their priorities straight and were wasting their welfare money on other things. Let the children be the victims, he seemed to be saying. Vander Zalm also declared that single mothers should go out and find jobs, despite his traditional view of the ideal family as one in which the father goes out to work while Mom stays home to look after the kids.

Throughout the first two years of Vander Zalm's administration, he and a number of cabinet ministers were faced with conflict-of-interest charges. The Premier revealed an astonishing lack of understanding of the issue, particularly in regard to his business and political relationship with entrepreneur Peter Toigo. Soon after taking office, in an obvious swipe at Bill Bennett's cabinet problems in this regard, he had promised to review the government's conflict guidelines. Two years later there was no sign of change, apparently because Vander Zalm has no clear idea of what constitutes conflict of interest. The existing guidelines have been described as vague and toothless.

By the end of his third year as premier in August of 1989, the public was seeing a different, subdued Vander Zalm. The smile had lost some of its glitter. No longer was the Premier as accessible or open-mouthed with the press. Painfully he had become aware that the job was "no piece of cake" as he had blithely described it in the beginning. His startling loss of popularity and accompanying plunge in the opinion polls has clearly taken some of the bounce out of his step. Vander Zalm had always preferred to wing it on his own; now the demands of politics and an edgy Social Credit party had forced the Premier to gag himself with public relations image-makers.

Every now and then, when he manages to break free of the reins, the results have been predictably disastrous. The most revealing outburst came at the low point in the government's fortunes in late 1988 when Vander Zalm attempted to plug his own cord into God, in the manner of W. A. C. Bennett. "It won't be easy," he said in a widely distributed talk to a Christian student seminar, "but good things weren't meant to be easy. Christ didn't have an easy way. He came into the world poor. He never travelled far from home. He was taunted and ridiculed. He never had a UBC education. He would have been low in the polls. But he left a tremendous impression on the world ..." Intended as a defense of his much criticized anti-abortion stand, Vander Zalm's outburst revealed instead a messianic view of his political career. Martyrdom for his beliefs may yet be his final refuge.

The most pressing issue for the government has become the need to somehow satisfy the growing environmental lobby for the preservation of the forests without creating unemployment and thereby crippling the valuable woods industry. Traditionally politicians have tried to keep a foot in each opposing camp, and the Vander Zalm administration has been no exception. Forest Minister Dave Parker, a heavy-handed former woodsman himself, spoke for the tree-cutters, while Vander Zalm expressed a new-found horror at the ravages of scorched-earth logging. It was a tough role for an old Socred used to pushing the economy for all it's worth and more. And it was even more unusual for a

British Columbia premier to suggest that there might be more to the job than salesmanship. Merely a passing fad, no doubt.

• • •

So what *does* the future hold for British Columbia? Is there any hope of joining the mainstream of Canadian politics or are we doomed to remain the laughing-stock of the country forever? Forecasts in this most unpredicable province are foolhardy, but significant change in the near future seems unlikely.

Alberta managed to make a smooth transition from Social Credit to Conservative governments, but the NDP was not a significant threat there. Liberals and Conservatives are blocked from regeneration in B.C. because of the certain knowledge that a split vote will result in an NDP government.

Obviously, a lot depends on the fate of the mercurial Bill Vander Zalm, a loose cannon on the political deck if there ever was one. He talks grandly of a ten-year economic plan for British Columbia, but is unlikely to be around long enough to see it through. It was said of Dave Barrett that he had "Neophyte's Disease, a malady characterized by excessive enthusiasms, unbounded faith, acute distortion of the priorities, and terminal shortness of sight. Seeing only programs and legislation, he ignored his own party." This could be Vander Zalm's political epitaph too.

If Vander Zalm stays on and takes Social Credit to its second defeat, the two mainline parties could regroup during an NDP administration. But the question as this is written is whether the accident-prone Vander Zalm can last out his term. The party's business supporters have let it be known that they are unhappy with the Premier's cockamamie style of government and have threatened to cut back on party funding. There will be strong pressure to replace Vander Zalm as leader before the next general election. NDP leader Mike Harcourt, described by one newspaper as a "relentlessly amiable moderate," can only watch and hope Social Credit self-destructs. For the rest of us, it will probably be politics as usual in this strangest of all provinces.

Bibliography

Books:

Akrigg, G.P.V. & Helen B. *British Columbia Chronicle, 1847-1871*. Discovery Press. Vancouver. 1977.

Barr, Robert. *The Measure of the Rule*. 1907. University of Toronto Press reprint. 1973.

Brock, Peter Jeffry. *Fighting Joe Martin*. National Press. Toronto. 1981.

Garr, Allen. *Tough Guy: Bill Bennett and the Taking of B.C.*. Key Porter. Toronto. 1985.

Jackman, S.W. *Portraits of the Premiers*. Gray's Publishing. Sidney. 1969.

___ *The Men at Cary Castle*. Victoria. 1972.

Kavic, Lorne J., and Nixon, Garry Brian. *The 1200 Days: A Shattered Dream; Dave Barrett and the NDP*. Kaen. Coquitlam. 1978.

Keate, Stuart. *Paper Boy*. Clarke, Irwin. Toronto. 1980.

Keene, Roger, and Humphreys, David C. *Conversations with W.A.C. Bennett*. Methuen. Toronto. 1980.

McGeer, Patrick L. *Politics in Paradise*. P. Martin & Assoc. Toronto. 1972.

Mitchell, David J. *W.A.C. Bennett and the Rise of British Columbia*. Douglas & McIntyre. Vancouver. 1983.

___ *Succession: The Political Reshaping of British Columbia*. Douglas & McIntyre. Vancouver. 1987.

Moore, Vincent. *Angelo Branca: Gladiator of the Courts*. Douglas & McIntyre. Vancouver. 1981.

Morley, J. Terence (et al). *The Reins of Power: Governing British Columbia*. Douglas and McIntyre. Vancouver. 1983.

Morton, James. *Honest John Oliver*. J.M. Dent. Toronto. 1933.

Ormsby, Margaret. *British Columbia: A History*. Macmillan. 1958.

Persky, Stan. *Son of Socred*. New Star. Vancouver. 1979.

____ *Bennett II*. New Star. Vancouver. 1983.

Ramsey, Bruce. *The PGE: Railway to the North*. Mitchell Press. Vancouver. 1962.

Robin, Martin. *The Rush for Spoils: The Company Province, 1871-1933*. McClelland & Stewart. Toronto. 1972.

____ *Pillars of Profit: The Company Province, 1934-1972*. McClelland & Stewart. Toronto. *1973*.

Saywell, John. *The Office of Lieutenant-Governor: A Study in Canadian Government and Politics*. University of Toronto Press. 1957.

Sherman, Paddy. *Bennett*. McClelland & Stewart. Toronto. 1966.

Smith, Dorothy B. Editor. *The Reminiscences of Doctor John Sebastian Helmcken*. University of B.C. Press. 1975.

Taylor, Geoffrey. *The Railway Contractors*. Victoria. 1988.

Thornhill, J.B. *British Columbia in the Making, 1913*. Constable. London. 1913.

Twigg, Alan. *Vander Zalm: From Immigrant to Premier*. Harbour. Madeira Park, B.C. 1986.

Walker, Russell. *Politicians of a Pioneer Province*. Mitchell Press. Vancouver. 1969.

Wild, Roland. *Amor De Cosmos*. Ryerson. Toronto. 1958.

Woodcock, George. *Amor De Cosmos: Journalist & Reformer*. Oxford. Toronto. 1975.

Worley, Ronald. *The Wonderful World of W.A.C. Bennett*. McClelland & Stewart. Toronto. 1972.

Articles:

Black, Edwin R. "British Columbia: The Politics of Exploitation." Reprinted in *Party Politics in Canada*, Hugh. G. Thorburn, Editor. Prentice- Hall. Toronto. 1972.

Hilliker, Gordon. "Fighting Joe Martin Comes to British Columbia." *The Advocate*. Vancouver Bar Association. September, 1987.

Unpublished:

Dailyde, Victor Kastytis. *The Administration of W.T. Bowser*. MA Thesis. University of Victoria. 1976.

Ross, Margaret. *Amor De Cosmos: A British Columbia Reformer*. MA Thesis. University of B.C. 1931.

Sanford, Thomas M. *The Politics of Protest: The Cooperative Commonwealth Federation and Social Credit League in British Columbia*. Phd Thesis. University of California. 1961.

Smith, Brian R.D. *Sir Richard McBride: A Study in the Conservative Party of British Columbia, 1903-1916*. MA Thesis. Queen's. 1959.

Sutherland, John Neil. *T.D. Pattullo: Party Leader*. MA Thesis. University of B.C. 1960.

Journals:

B.C. Studies
B.C. Historical Quarterly
Canadian Annual Review
Canadian Historical Review
Pacific Northwest Quarterly
Victoria Historical Review

Magazines:

Canadian Forum
Equity
Maclean's
Saturday Night

Newspapers:

Toronto Globe & Mail
Toronto Star
Vancouver Province
Vancouver Sun
Victoria Colonist
Victoria Times

Index